The Man Pulled a Gun on Mark and Cara. . . .

He pointed the pistol at Cara's head. "I'll bet if I shoot one of you, the other one will suddenly remember where your parents are. Shall we try it?"

"No!" Cara screamed.

He moved the gun toward Mark. "One of you is going to tell me."

"But our parents are missing!" Mark cried. "We don't know where they are!"

"Which one of you should I shoot?" he asked. "It's too bad, but you're leaving me no choice. I have to shoot one of you."

He moved the pistol back and forth, first pointing it at Cara, then at Mark.

"I think I'll shoot Mark," he said. "Good-bye, Mark." He lowered the pistol toward Mark's head.

Mark closed his eyes and waited.

One second. Two seconds. Three seconds.

How much would it hurt? Would he really feel it? Would he know when he was hit?

Four seconds. Five seconds. Six . . .

Books by R. L. Stine

Available from ARCHWAY Paperbacks

FEAR STREET

R·L·STINE

Missing

AN ARCHWAY PAPERBACK
Published by POCKET BOOKS
New York   London   Toronto   Sydney   Tokyo   Singapore

This book is a work of fiction. Names, characters, places and incidents are either the product of the author's imagination or are used fictitiously. Any resemblance to actual events or locales or persons, living or dead, is entirely coincidental.

AN ARCHWAY PAPERBACK *Original*

An Archway Paperback published by
POCKET BOOKS, a division of Simon & Schuster Inc.
1230 Avenue of the Americas, New York, NY 10020

Copyright © 1990 by Parachute Press, Inc.
Cover art copyright © 1990 Gabrielle

All rights reserved, including the right to reproduce
this book or portions thereof in any form whatsoever.
For information address Pocket Books, 1230 Avenue
of the Americas, New York, NY 10020

ISBN: 0-671-69410-3

First Archway Paperback printing January 1990

15 14 13 12 11 10 9 8 7

Fear Street is a registered trademark of Parachute Press, Inc.

AN ARCHWAY PAPERBACK and colophon are
registered trademarks of Simon & Schuster Inc.

Printed in the U.S.A.

IL 6+

chapter

1

The first night Mom and Dad didn't come home, Mark and I weren't terribly upset about it. In fact, we had a party.

It didn't start out to be a party. We were feeling kind of lonely, so Mark invited Gena over. Then I called my new friends from school, Lisa and Shannon. And they invited some kids, and before we knew it, there were about twenty of us partying all over the large living room that was still so new and uncomfortable to Mark and me.

We had just moved in two months before at the beginning of September, just in time to start school at Shadyside High. And even though the house was twice as roomy as our old house in Brookline, it was older and kind of run-down.

The kids we met at school always acted surprised when we said we lived on Fear Street. They were always telling us stories about horrible things that happened around Fear Street and in the thick woods that ran behind the houses—stories about strange creatures, unexplained disappearances, ghosts, and weird howls and stuff.

I think Mark believed the stories. He always believes everything people tell him. Even though my brother is a year older than I am, I think I'm a lot more cynical than he is.

Mark is just a straightforward guy. I mean, what you see is what you get. Sure, he looks like a jock with those broad shoulders and the big neck, the blond, wavy hair, and those green eyes, the cute dimple in his chin that he hates to be teased about. But he isn't dumb or anything. He just trusts people. He never kids other people, and I don't think he realizes it when other people are putting him on.

Mark makes friends in a hurry. Kids like him right away. I think my sense of humor, my cynical way of looking at the world turns some kids off. So most of the people at the party were new friends Mark had made at Shadyside in the two months we'd been going there.

I'd become pretty good friends with Lisa and Shannon, who were in my homeroom. But we weren't exactly best buddies yet. And I certainly hadn't found a guy I was interested in—not the way Mark had found Gena Rawlings.

Gena was the reason for the big fight at our breakfast table that morning. Yeah, Mark had a big blowout with Mom and Dad before school. Mom and Dad just didn't approve of Gena, and they didn't want Mark to see her. He was seeing a *lot* of Gena. I mean, like, every day. They were what you could call inseparable. It was kind of sweet, really. Mark is always really intense, but I don't think he ever felt so intense about a girl.

So when he asked Mom and Dad what it was they didn't like about Gena, and they couldn't really tell him, he just blew up.

He had good reason, I think. Mom and Dad are pretty smart people, and they've always been really good at saying what's on their minds. So what was their reason for disliking Gena?

"It's gonna hurt your schoolwork," Dad said. Pretty lame. Mark has always had a solid B average. He works really hard in school, much harder than I do, and takes it as seriously as he takes everything else.

So I don't blame Mark for jumping all over Dad for that one. Of course Dad started screaming back and said a lot of things he shouldn't have. Which forced Mark to turn real red in the face and scream a lot of things *he* shouldn't have. And then Mom got into it, and it got so noisy I thought the peeling yellow kitchen walls might crack and fall!

I just slumped down in my seat and stared at my Pop-Tart. The strawberry stuff was oozing out onto the plate. I didn't really feel like eating breakfast, anyway. I'm not that crazy about Gena, but I don't think Mom and Dad had any business giving Mark a hard time about her—at least not first thing in the morning when we were trying to have breakfast.

It was the worst screaming match we'd had in a long time. The last one, I guess, was back in Brookline, when Mark and I borrowed the car without telling our parents, and they reported it stolen. We were both grounded for two months for that little episode. No big deal.

But this one *was* a big deal to Mark. "I'm sixteen. I know what I'm doing!" he screamed.

Mom and Dad laughed, which was a really horrible thing to do.

Mark was really furious now. He picked up his Pop-Tart and started to throw it across the room. I pictured it hitting the wall with a *splat*. I'm really bad.

But Mark stopped himself just in time and instead tossed it back onto his plate, turned, and stomped out the kitchen door, slamming it as hard as he could behind him. The window glass in the old door shook inside its frame, but it didn't fall out.

Mom and Dad had gone very pale. They looked at each other across the table and shook their heads, but didn't say anything. "You'll be late for school," Dad said to me a while later. His voice sounded shaky. I guess the screaming had him really upset.

Our parents had both been really nervous ever since we moved to Shadyside. I figured it was just the strain of moving and everything—although they should be used to it. Because of their work, we move all the time. We've lived in six different places in the last eight years.

That's not easy on them—or on Mark and me. I've always found it hard to make real friends knowing that in a year or so I'd be moving away and leaving them behind. My mom puts me down a lot for being a loner, but what choice do I have? I mean, why get involved with people when you're only going to know them for a short while?

Anyway, I got my book bag and looked out the

kitchen window. There was Mark, a scowl on his face, in the backyard with his bow, shooting arrows one after the other into a poor, defenseless maple tree.

My brother is an archery freak. The first thing he did when we moved here—even before he took a look at his room—was to search out the right tree in the backyard to hang his target. He's really very good at it. He's a great shot, but of course he should be when you consider the hours and hours he spends doing it.

"It's a good way to let out your frustrations," he always tells me. I guess he was pretty frustrated this morning because he was looking really intense, even for him, shooting an arrow and not even looking at where it went before pulling another from the sheath.

"He's going to shoot his eye out one day," Mom always complains. Sometimes she tries extra hard, I think, to sound like a mom because it doesn't come naturally to her. She's pretty young and pretty cool. And when she's home—which isn't very often because of work—she's a lot of fun to be with.

Dad's okay, too, although he's very serious and intense—like Mark. Sometimes I think he's really hard to talk to. It's like he always seems to have something else on his mind. But maybe that's just my problem.

Anyway, we don't have too many fights like the one this morning. We get along pretty well, I think. Or maybe it's just that Mom and Dad are away at work so much, we don't have time to fight.

I grabbed Mark's jacket and book bag, ran out the back door, and somehow managed to pull him to the bus stop. We didn't even say good-bye to Mom and Dad.

We didn't realize that it might be the last time we ever saw them.

"What's wrong with Gena, anyway?" Mark asked as we waited for the South Side bus.

"Maybe they think she's too short for you," I joked. Gena *was* about a foot shorter than Mark.

"Huh?"

"Just joking," I muttered. Why do I always have to tell Mark when I'm joking?

Gena was short, but to put it bluntly (which I'm good at), she had a great bod. She also was really pretty, with long, straight black hair down to her waist, creamy white skin without a blemish, and beautiful black eyes that absolutely drove boys crazy. All of the guys at school think Gena is really sexy—and she is.

Now, at ten o'clock at night, with no Mom and Dad around and with the impromptu party in full swing in our living room, there was sexy Gena sitting on my brother's lap on the sofa.

I thought about the fight that morning, and I looked at my watch and wondered where Mom and Dad could be. They usually called if they were going to be late at work.

The CD player was really cranked up. Someone was playing some heavy metal group at top volume. Lisa's boyfriend Cory was having a tug-of-war over a can of soda with some guy I'd never seen before. The can seemed to explode in their hands, a foam of soda erupting over the living-room carpet.

Oh, please, I thought, don't let this party get out of control.

Mom and Dad should be home any minute. And then . . .

I looked back to the sofa at Mark and Gena. She had her hands wrapped around his neck and she was leaning down over him and kissing him, her eyes closed. It was quite a kiss.

I didn't mean to stare—but give me a break! *You could be arrested in some states for a kiss like that!* I told myself.

And then I thought I heard the front doorbell.

There was loud laughter in the corner by the den. Gena and Mark didn't move. They were in their own world. No one else seemed to hear it.

I ran to the living-room window and looked out. There was a big blue Chevy Caprice in the driveway. Twisting my head against the glass, I could see a tall man wearing a dark shirt and wrinkled chinos standing under the porch light. He saw me peering out at him and held up a badge, a police badge.

Surrounded by all the music and noise and laughter, I suddenly went numb. My heart seemed to stop. Everything seemed to stop.

I knew why the policeman had come.

Something terrible had happened to Mom and Dad.

chapter

2

*T*he policeman smiled as I pulled open the door. "Good evening," he said, looking me up and down.

The porch light sent a glare onto the screen door, and it took me a while to focus on his face. He wasn't young. There were streaks of gray on his mustache. He was staring hard at me through the screen door with the coldest blue eyes I've ever seen, icy blue like a frozen lake in winter. "I'm Captain Farraday," he said.

"What's wrong?" I asked. "My mom and dad—are they—"

"Are they home?" he asked, and he smiled, revealing straight white teeth.

"No. They—"

"They're not here?"

"No. They're working late, I think."

He stared past me into the hallway.

"You didn't come to tell me something about them?" I asked, feeling relieved.

He didn't seem to understand the question. "No. Uh . . . I'm investigating a burglary in this neighborhood."

"A burglary?"

"Yeah. Three houses down. I'm going house to house, seeing if anybody saw anything suspicious. You know, a strange car or something."

"Oh. Well . . . no, I haven't see anything."

A burst of laughter from the living room was followed by a crash of shattering glass. The heavy metal music sounded even louder here in the hallway.

"You notice anyone on the street? You know, anyone you haven't seen before?" His blue eyes stared into mine.

I looked away. "No. No one. I never see too many people on this street, Captain. We're pretty new in the neighborhood, so—"

"Expecting your parents soon?"

"Probably. I don't know. Sometimes they work really late."

We stared at each other for a long moment. Then he reached into the shirt pocket of his uniform and pulled out a little white card. "Here. Take this." He opened the screen door and handed me the card. "It's got my special direct line on it. If you see anything suspicious, call me—anytime."

I took the card and thanked him.

"Keep it near your phone," he said. "Just in case the burglar decides to try this neighborhood again." Then he turned and stepped off the porch.

I stood there listening to his boots crunch over the gravel driveway. I watched him climb into his big old Chevy. I wondered why he wasn't driving a police car.

"He must use it to trap speeders," I told myself. The big car didn't make a sound as it pulled off the curb and disappeared into the night.

I shoved the card into my jeans pocket and walked back into the living room. It struck me that the room was suddenly very quiet. I glanced over to the sofa. Gena was still in Mark's lap, but she had turned around to face me. Both of them were staring at me. Someone had turned the music down.

"I'm really sorry, Cara," Cory Brooks, Lisa's boyfriend, said quietly. He looked very upset.

"What?"

What on earth is going on? I wondered. What happened in here while I was talking to Captain Farraday?

"I was just clowning around with David Metcalfe over there, and I guess I . . . well . . . I wasn't feeling too well, and I guess I got a little sick."

I glanced over at Mark, but he had his face buried in Gena's hair.

Then I saw it. A disgusting puddle of green-and-brown vomit dripping down over the side of the coffee table.

"Nice move, ace," Cory's friend David muttered from against the wall.

"Ohh, I'm gonna be sick, too," a girl I'd never seen before groaned, covering her mouth with her hands.

"I'll help you clean it up," Cory said, looking really embarrassed.

"That's okay. Just get a spoon," I told him. "I'll eat it before it clots!"

"Ohh! Total gross-out!" Gena cried.

I bent down and picked up the phony rubber vomit. And then I heaved it at Cory.

Everyone laughed. Cory looked really disappointed.

I had believed it was real for a few seconds, but I'd never give him the satisfaction of telling him that.

"Cory, what a nerdy thing to do," Lisa said, giving him a hard shove on the shoulder.

Cory is big and solid. Her shove didn't move him. "It was David's idea," he said, laughing. He tossed the disgusting rubber joke at his friend.

"I think we should end the party on this high note," I said. A lot of kids groaned in protest. My brother had wrapped his arms around Gena and was nuzzling her neck. I could see that he was going to be no help at all.

"Come on. It's a school night. And the police were already here once."

They all uttered cries of surprise. They were so busy partying, they hadn't even noticed the policeman at the door.

"My parents will be home any minute," I said. I hoped that wasn't a lie. I was beginning to get worried about them. It was nearly eleven.

Kids reluctantly started to leave. I said good night to Lisa and Shannon. They were the only friends I had actually invited, and I hadn't had two seconds to talk to them.

I noticed a big wet stain on the edge of the carpet. This one was real, not rubber. "Oh, well. It's good for the carpet," I muttered to myself.

From the front entranceway, I watched everyone head down the front lawn to their cars, laughing and joking.

"See you tomorrow."

"Not if I see you first."

I hoped the grouchy neighbor down the block was enjoying all the shouting and loud laughter.

Feeling a little chilled, I closed the front door and walked back to the living room, rubbing the sleeves of my sweatshirt to get warm. I couldn't believe it—Mark and Gena hadn't moved from the couch!

I'm gonna have to turn a hose on them! I thought.

"Hey, guys," I said, raising my wrist and taking a long look at my Swatch. A subtle hint.

The two lovebirds ignored me.

"How's Gena going to get home?" I asked.

Mark actually looked up at me. "I'll drive her," he said. He had lipstick smeared all around his mouth. He looked like Bozo the Clown.

"In what?" I asked. "Mom and Dad took the car to work, remember?"

"Oh." He thought about it. An evil smile spread across his usually innocent-looking face. "I guess she'll have to spend the night."

"You pig!" Gena laughed, and tried to smother him with one of the crushed-velvet sofa pillows. They started wrestling around as if I weren't even there.

Maybe Mom and Dad are right about her, I thought, feeling annoyed—and jealous—at the same time. Why didn't I have some guy to wrestle around with and act like a jerk with? A loud knock on the door interrupted my peevish thoughts.

"That's probably Mom and Dad," I said, just to scare Mark and Gena.

It didn't work. "Why would they knock?" Mark asked.

I ran to answer the door. It was Cory Brooks. "I forgot my vomit," he said a little sheepishly.

He followed me into the living room. He searched for a while, then found his treasured item under a chair cushion. He carefully folded it up and stuffed it into the pocket of his jeans jacket.

"Hey, Cory, can I have a ride home?" Gena was actually standing up. She straightened her blue cashmere sweater, which had become twisted.

"Sure. If you don't mind riding in the backseat with Metcalfe."

Gena made a face. "Maybe I'll walk."

"Don't sweat it. I'll tie him up with the seat belts," Cory said. She followed him out the door after standing up on tiptoes to give Mark a last long, lingering kiss.

A few seconds later, Mark and I were alone in the cluttered living room. "You'd better wash the lipstick off your face," I told him, trying not to laugh at how ridiculous he looked. "Then we've got to clean up."

He didn't say anything, just hurried off to wash away the evidence. He came back to the living room a few minutes later, looking somewhat dazed.

As I said, he'd never had a girlfriend like Gena before. I was going to say something to him about it, but of course I didn't. Brothers and sisters can't really talk about stuff like that. Only on TV. In all the sitcoms, brothers and sisters have these long, serious heart-to-hearts. Then they hug each other and go to the kitchen for snacks.

But it isn't that way in real life. If Mark ever hugged me, I'd call a doctor!

"Some party," he said, shaking his head. I think he actually looked a little guilty. "How are we gonna clean all this up?"

"Quickly," I said. "Before Mom and Dad walk in and see it."

"I don't think they're coming home tonight," he said, picking some crushed cans up off the floor.

"Huh? Of course they are."

"It wouldn't be the first time." He sounded a little bitter. "I'll get a big trash bag in the kitchen."

I stood there, suddenly feeling very tired, listening to the old floorboards in the hall squeak as he walked to the kitchen. He was right about Mom and Dad. This wouldn't be the first time they had stayed out all night, either working or partying.

As I said, my parents were young and didn't really like the idea of having to act like parents. I'm not putting them down. They were perfectly good parents, more fun than most when they were around. But they just didn't take being parents as seriously as most other parents did.

They found a lot of other things more important. Their work, for example. I don't completely understand what they do. They're mainframe computer specialists. That means they go into huge companies and install enormous computer systems for them. It takes months, sometimes years. Then they move on to another big corporation, often in another city.

That's why we move so much.

And wherever we move, Mom and Dad get involved in all kinds of things—community things, I mean. You know, clubs and organizations of all kinds. Sometimes I have to admit that I feel hurt that they immediately rush out and find all these clubs to join. I mean, it's like they don't want to stay home and spend time with Mark and me.

But now that I'm older, I realize that's silly. And selfish. They have the right to their own lives, their own interests.

But they could at least call and tell us when they're going to be out late, couldn't they?

Mark came back, carrying a large green plastic trash bag. "I'll hold the bag. Just dump everything in," he said, and yawned.

"How come I never get to hold the bag?" I complained, not really serious.

"What if something happened to them?" he asked, suddenly sounding worried.

"Huh?"

"What if they were in an accident or something?"

"If they were in an accident, they'd call," I said. It was a standard joke between us. Only it wasn't very funny tonight.

"What if the car stalled on Fear Street, back in the woods, and they're lost in the woods? You know those stories about how people go into the woods and come out looking different and not remembering who they are."

"Who told you that story?" I asked, making a face.

"Cory Brooks. He said it was in the newspaper."

"That's about as funny as his rubber vomit. He was putting you on, Mark."

He didn't say anything for a while. But I knew the look on his face. It was his worried face. I'd seen that look a lot. Someone has to be the worrier in every family, and in our family it was Mark.

"Stop looking like that," I told him.

"Looking like what?"

"Looking like that. If you keep looking like that, I'll start to worry, too."

"Let's call them," he said.

"Yeah. Okay." Why hadn't I thought of that sooner?

I followed Mark into the kitchen. We had their number written down on a pad by the phone. It didn't go through the switchboard. It was a direct line right to their office, so we could call it at any hour of the day.

"You call," Mark said, leaning against the Formica counter. He looked very worried.

"Sure," I said. I leafed through the pad till I found the office number. Then I pulled the receiver off the wall and started to dial. Then I stopped.

"What's wrong?" Mark asked.

"There's no dial tone," I told him.

The phone was completely dead.

chapter

3

We both stood there staring at the phone, as if it were going to come to life or something. "That's weird," Mark said finally. "Why is it out? There hasn't been a storm or anything."

"Well, at least that explains why Mom and Dad haven't called," I said. "They couldn't!"

I put the silent receiver back. We were both smiling, feeling a little less worried. Mark started to say something, but stopped.

We both heard the sound. Footsteps above our head. The ceiling creaked.

Someone was walking around upstairs.

I caught the look of fear on Mark's face as the footsteps pounded down the front stairs. I probably looked just as frightened.

We stood listening to the padding sounds grow louder. And then he walked into the kitchen.

And we saw that it was only Roger.

I laughed out loud. Mark was still too shaken to

laugh. He was sweating bullets, and he'd become about the same color as the faded gray wallpaper, which made me laugh even harder. I was so relieved.

How could we have forgotten about Roger?

Well, he was so quiet and so *invisible* most of the time, it was easy to forget about him.

Roger was a distant cousin of my mother's, and he was boarding with us. He had arrived a few days after we moved in at Fear Street, and my parents told him he could have the attic room all to himself. This was pretty funny, actually, because the attic room is so small, two people couldn't squeeze into it. Roger *had* to have it all to himself!

Even Roger by himself didn't quite fit into the room. He's so tall, and the ceiling slants at such a low angle, he has to stoop when he stands up in there. But he has a bed and a desk, and he seems pretty happy living with us.

We don't really see him that much. Mark and I try to be friendly. He *is* a relative, after all, and since we move around so much, we're kinda lonely for relatives.

But Roger is hard to get to know. He's so quiet. He's the shyest person I ever met, I think. He's really handsome. He has sandy brown hair and dark, intense eyes. He looks just like a model in a magazine, but I don't think he has any idea how good-looking he is. He's just so shy. He goes to the junior college in the next town. So he spends most of his time up in the attic studying and writing papers.

I don't really know why Mom and Dad took him in. It can't be for the rent he pays. We really don't need the money. Strangely enough, he isn't the first boarder we've had. Other young guys have boarded with us in other towns we've lived in. I guess Mom and Dad just like to help college students out.

"Hi, Roger. You scared us," Mark said, the color starting to return to his face.

A look of alarm crossed Roger's handsome face. "Sorry. Didn't mean to."

Mark and I headed back to the living room to clean up, and Roger followed. "When did you come in?" I asked, starting to gather up soda and beer cans that littered the room.

"Little while ago. I heard all the noise, so—"

"You should've joined the party," Mark said, holding open the trash bag and following me around the room.

"No, that's okay." Roger looked embarrassed for some reason. It must be hard to be that shy. I couldn't picture Roger at a party. I tried to imagine him dancing. He was so stiff and uptight, he probably never danced.

He bent down and grabbed a handful of goldfish pretzels from a bowl beside the sofa. "I was going to do some reading, but I wanted to ask your parents something."

"They're not home," I told him.

He looked very surprised. He looked at his watch.

"Did they mention to you they'd be working late?" I asked him.

"No." He shook his head. He scratched his chin. "Well, no big deal. I guess I can ask them later."

He tossed some of the goldfish into his mouth. "You guys okay?"

"Yeah. Sure," I told him.

He gathered up some paper plates and stuffed them into the trash bag Mark was holding.

"They stay out late a lot," Mark said.

"They called?" Roger asked, reaching for another handful of the goldfish.

"No. The phone's broken."

"Huh? That's weird. Your parents leave a note?"

"No, but I'm sure they're just working late," I said. "Sometimes they get so caught up with their computer problems they lose track of the time."

"Sometimes they work twenty-four hours straight," Mark added, taking a long drink from someone's half-empty soda can, tilting it over his mouth till soda trickled down his chin.

"You're a pig," I told him.

"Hey—I'm thirsty!"

"So they didn't leave a note or anything?" Roger asked, sounding impatient. I wondered why he was asking so many questions. It really wasn't like him. I guess he wanted to see my parents about something important.

"No. They might be at one of their club meetings," Mark said, crushing the soda can in his hand and tossing it into the trash bag.

"They usually come home for dinner before their club meetings," I said.

"Did you look in their room?" Roger asked.

"Huh? What for?" Even Mark was becoming suspicious. This was very strange behavior for Roger.

Roger blushed. "You know. To see if they left a note or anything."

"They always leave notes on the refrigerator," I told him. "You know Mom and Dad. They're computer people, right? They do everything by a system, everything the same way all the time."

It's true. My parents like to think they're such free spirits. But you should see them if I put the Frosted Flakes back in the wrong cabinet!

Roger yawned and stretched. He's good-looking even when he yawns, I thought. "Guess I'll talk to them tomorrow." He grabbed another handful of goldfish, nearly emptying the bowl, and turned toward the stairs. "G'night."

"Night," Mark and I called, and looked at each other.

"He's weird," Mark said.

"He's Mom's cousin, so he *has* to be weird," I cracked. "He certainly seemed nervous tonight."

"Yeah. He looked like he wanted to borrow money or something."

"Maybe you're right," I said, suddenly feeling really tired. "He did look like he wanted *something*. Where are you going?" Mark was heading into the den.

"It's almost twelve. Thought I'd watch 'Star Trek.' "

"Mark, you've seen them all ten times!"

"No. These are the new ones. I've only seen them twice."

Mark is a real "Star Trek" freak. He watches the reruns whenever they're on, usually after midnight. He isn't much of a reader, but he reads all the *Star Trek* novels as soon as they come out. He thinks it's hilarious to give me the Vulcan salute when no one's watching. Like I said, my brother doesn't have much of a sense of humor.

21

"Maybe we *should* take a look in Mom and Dad's room," I said.

He gave me a funny look. "You okay?"

"Yeah, I know. It's not like me to be a worrier. I just have a weird feeling about this, you know."

"Okay. Let me just see what episode they're showing." He plopped down on the leather couch, picked up the remote control, and clicked on the TV.

I sat down wearily on the arm of the couch, too tired to do any more cleaning up. A few minutes later, "Star Trek" came on.

"It's an old one," Mark said, "but it's pretty neat. Kirk, Uhura, and Chekov get captured, and the guys that captured them make them wear these dog collars and train for combat."

"Thrills," I said. I'm not into "Star Trek." "Come on. Let's go upstairs and check out Mom and Dad's room."

"Oh, all right." He aimed the remote control and turned off the TV. "Help me up." He raised his arms over his head and expected me to pull him up.

"No way," I told him. "You weigh a ton."

He looked hurt. Groaning, he pulled himself to his feet. We were both really tired. It was nearly one o'clock in the morning and we had to get up in six hours to go to school.

I followed Mark out of the den and up the stairs. I hated the way the old wooden steps creaked and squeaked when we stepped on them. Mom and Dad were going to get carpet for the stairs, but they just didn't have time.

Our house in Brookline had been brand-new. It was hard to get used to all the creepy noises an old house like this one made. I'm not a nervous person. Mark is the nervous one in the family. But I always have the feeling that someone else is in the room, or someone is coming down the stairs, or someone is creeping up behind me—all because of the creaks and groans and weird noises the house makes.

I guess I'll get used to it. But I do have to admit, I feel a lot more comfortable in this run-down old house when Mom and Dad are home.

Where could they be? I wondered.

Their bedroom door was closed. That wasn't unusual. They often closed it when they went out. Neat and tidy. Everything in its place. Everything in perfect order.

I turned the knob and pushed open the door.

I was surprised to see light. A lamp on the far bed table had been left on.

"Oh!"

I didn't mean to scream. A noise frightened me. It was just a window shade flapping in the wind against the open window.

Then I saw their bed and cried out again.

It was obvious that something terrible had happened. . . .

chapter

4

I'm not sure why my sister went bananas. What's the matter with her, anyway! She never saw an unmade bed before? I mean, give me a break. Sure, Mom and Dad are neat freaks, and sure they *always* made their bed before going to work. But one unmade bed is no reason to freak out and start screaming that something terrible has happened!

I got Cara calmed down in my usual way. I yelled at her and told her to shut up. I mean, I saw right away that there was nothing to be so pushed out of shape about.

Hey, I'm supposed to be the worrier in the family. Cara's supposed to be the calm, cool, and collected one. Well, she was blowing her whole image, that's for sure.

"I'm sorry," she said, biting her lower lip the way she always does when she's done something wrong, which is most of the time. "I didn't mean to scream like that. It's just . . . just—"

"Just what?" I asked. I wasn't going to let her off the hook so easily. I mean, she scared the you-know-what out of me when she screamed like that.

Her voice got tiny and soft. "I guess it was the way the bedspread is half on the floor and the sheet is all balled up like that. It—it just looked like there's been a fight or something."

"You've got to chill out," I told her, sitting down on the edge of the bed. "I don't know what's got you so shook. I mean, you act like Mom and Dad have never stayed out late before."

Cara was so worked up, I decided I had to act supercalm. I was a little worried, too, but I decided not to let Cara know. Actually, I was worried and I was glad. I was glad they had stayed out late because that meant I could invite Gena over, and Gena was really h-o-t tonight!

Sitting on the unmade bed, I thought about the big fight I'd had with Mom and Dad that morning. What was their problem, anyway? Gena was a fox! She was real smart, too, and nice, and she really likes me—a lot. I've only met her dad a few times, but he seems like a good guy. I think he's a doctor. So what is Mom and Dad's problem? Why the big objection to my seeing Gena?

It was so strange how they couldn't give any reasons.

Mom and Dad are always real big with the reasons. They always have at least two or three reasons for everything they do. They're always putting Gena and me down for doing something just because we felt like doing it and then not being able to explain why we did it.

Like everything in life should have a reason, right?

So when I asked their reason for telling me not to see Gena, all they could say was, "Trust us. We know more than you do about things."

What kind of reason is that? Trust us!

I suppose I shouldn't have lost my cool the way I did. But they're used to me blowing my stack. Besides, I had good reason. For once, I was right.

Of course, I realized, sitting in their room, if something terrible had happened to them, I'd feel pretty bad about having had a fight with them this morning. But I shook away that thought. No point in thinking like that. It wouldn't do anyone any good.

"They've worked very late before," I told Cara.

"They usually call." She didn't look any calmer. She was standing over me with her arms crossed over her sweatshirt. "I know, I know. The phone is busted. But they could've called and left a message with Mrs. Fisher next door, couldn't they?"

"Cara, you've got to stop this worrying," I said. "It's just not like you."

But instead of listening to me, she suddenly let out a little gasp. Her mouth dropped open and her eyes grew wide with fright.

I realized she wasn't looking at me. She was looking past me to the window. "Mark—" Her voice came out a whisper. She leaned forward and grabbed my shoulder. Her fingers gripped my sweater. "Mark . . . there's someone—"

"Huh?" I really couldn't hear her.

She pushed my shoulder until I spun around. At first I couldn't see what had frightened her. I saw the window, which was half-open. I saw the darkness beyond the window and a narrow sliver of pale white moon. I saw the patterned floor-length curtains billow a little from the gusting night breeze.

And then I saw them. The two shoes sticking out from under the curtain to the right of the window.

Suddenly I understood my sister's sudden fright—and felt it myself. I stared at the shoes beneath the curtain and at the slight bulge that made the curtain appear to blow in the wind.

And I realized—as Cara did—that someone else was there with us in our parents' bedroom.

chapter
5

*I*f I had thought about it, I probably wouldn't have done it. But, like I said, I don't always have reasons for the things I do. Sometimes I just do them. Then I think up my reasons later, when it's too late.

Anyway, I jumped off the bed. And I ran toward the window.

I could hear Cara yelling to me to stop. But it was too late. I couldn't stop now.

I don't know what I thought I was going to do. I was feeling more anger than fear. I know that. I mean, what was someone doing in our parents' room like that, hiding behind the curtain?

Was it a burglar?

I didn't stop to think that it might be someone really dangerous. I didn't stop to think that it might be someone who would blow me away just as soon as look at me. I guess I didn't think at all.

I just ran—and then stopped when Roger stepped

out from behind the curtains, looking real embarrassed.

"It's only me," he said. I guess he saw the fierce look on my face. He held up both hands, as if surrendering.

"Roger! What were you doing there?" Cara cried.

"Uh . . . just looking out the window. I . . . uh . . . thought I heard something outside, but it was just a dog or something."

"But what are you doing in here?" I asked, my heart still pounding.

"You really scared us," Cara said angrily, crossing her arms over her chest.

"Sorry. I just came in to see if your parents left a note or something. Then I went to the window when I heard something outside. I didn't hear you come in."

I believed him, but Cara seemed to have her doubts. My sister never believes anything anyone tells her. "But how could you not hear us? We were talking and everything."

"I . . . uh . . . guess those curtains are very heavy. They keep out the sound," Roger said. He pushed a hand through his wavy brown hair. He was sweating. It was hot in our parents' room, but not *that* hot.

"I really didn't mean to scare you," Roger said, looking past me to Cara. She still had her arms wrapped tightly in front of her. "I was just concerned about your parents and—"

"What's that in your hand?" Cara interrupted.

Roger held up a small black box. "This? It's just my Walkman." He started toward the door.

"No headphones?" Cara asked suspiciously.

"I . . . uh . . . left them upstairs," Roger said. He put the Walkman into his pants pocket.

The window curtains suddenly billowed out into the room.

All three of us cried out in surprise.

They had just been blown by the wind. Somewhere down the street in the Fear Street woods, an animal howled. I had a sudden chill. Guys at school had told me stories about wolves that roamed wild in the woods behind our house.

"Really. I'm sorry if I scared you two," Roger repeated, yawning. "Guess we're all pretty tired." He was halfway out the door, then turned around. "Listen, don't worry about your mom and dad. I'm sure they'll be back when you wake up in the morning."

"Yeah. Probably," Cara said. Her shoulders slumped and she let out a loud sigh. "Sorry if we frightened *you*," she added, making peace with Roger. "We didn't know it was you."

"Night."

"Good night."

Roger disappeared out the door. We listened to his footsteps as he climbed the stairs to his room up in the attic. Then Cara dived onto the bed, sliding on her stomach and burying her face in Mom's pillow.

I walked over and closed the window. Down on the ground the wind was swirling the dead leaves across the front yard. Something on the street caught my eye. It was a gray van, parked directly across from our house. I hadn't remembered seeing it there before. There was no writing on the side. It was too dark to see if anyone was in it or not.

What was it doing there?

I pulled the heavy curtains closed and stepped away.

"Think Roger was telling the truth?" Cara asked, her voice muffled because her face was still buried in the pillow.

"I don't know. Maybe," I said. "Why wouldn't he be?"

"He looked so embarrassed."

"You'd be embarrassed, too," I said. "He felt stupid, that's all."

I don't know why I was defending Roger. I had nothing against him, but I didn't really like him all that much. We didn't have anything in common. That was part of the problem. He wasn't into sports and I wasn't into nineteenth-century English lit. He was so good-looking. Too good-looking, I thought. Cara's girl-friends always started giggling and carrying on whenever Roger walked into the room. Maybe I was just a little jealous.

But I really didn't understand why we needed him around. Sure, he was a distant cousin or something. But that didn't mean he had to live with us, did it? It made me uncomfortable to have someone else in the house. The creepy old house was uncomfortable enough as it was, especially compared to the neat house we'd had back in Brookline. We didn't need some college guy lurking about, hiding behind the curtains.

So I don't know why I was taking Roger's side. I guess it's because I just like to argue with Cara.

"What was he looking for in here?" she asked, rolling onto her back, her face hidden in the fat pillow.

"Same thing we were, I guess," I said, walking over

and sitting down at the far end of the big queen-size platform bed.

"But if he was looking for a note, why was he hiding behind the drapes, staring out the window?"

I groaned. Cara could be really exhausting sometimes. "Give me a break. He explained it, didn't he? What do you want me to say?"

"You're right. I'm just tired." She closed her eyes.

"You're going to sleep here?"

She yawned. "No. I'm getting up." She stretched out her arms and smiled. It was a very comfortable bed.

"See ya," I said. I thought about Gena. I wondered if it was too late to call her. Probably. I thought maybe I'd call anyway.

Suddenly the smile dropped from Cara's face. She sat up quickly.

"What is it?"

"I found something under the sheet."

She had a small object in her hand. It looked like a tiny, white skull. I walked over to get a closer look. "What is it? A human skull?"

"No." Cara held it up close to her face to examine it in the dim lamplight. "It's . . . it's a monkey."

"What?"

She held it up and turned it around so I could see it better. It was a carved, white monkey's head about the size of a Ping-Pong ball. There were rhinestones deep in the eye sockets. They glowed yellow in the light from the bed-table lamp.

I took it from her and rolled it around between my fingers. "Strange. It feels so cold."

"I know," Cara said, and I could see a flash of fear cross her face. "There's something creepy about it."

I held it up and turned it so that it was facing me. As I stared into its shimmering eyes, it seemed to stare back into mine. It was carved ivory, the monkey's twin nostrils deep and dark, its teeth pulled back the width of its face in an ugly, frightening grin. It was so smooth, so cold.

And those rhinestone eyes seemed to peer into mine—seemed to radiate—what?—radiate evil!

I know, I know. Maybe all those rotten horror flicks Cara and I have rented have rotted my brain. Maybe I was just tired. Maybe I was upset because Mom and Dad weren't home.

But there was something ugly, something evil, about that tiny white monkey skull, about those strange, sparkling eyes, about that frozen monkey grin.

I stared at it as if hypnotized for the longest time. Then I couldn't stand it any longer, and I wrapped my fingers around the mysterious object, buried it in my hand, and shut my eyes. Even though I had been holding it tightly, it remained ice-cold, the cold burning my hand the way dry ice can burn. I tossed it back to Cara, who looked at it again, then tossed it onto the bed table, her face filled with disgust.

"What is it? Where did it come from?" she asked.

Just two more questions that I couldn't answer that night.

chapter
6

I didn't sleep well that night. Big surprise. I stared up at the shadows crisscrossing the ceiling, thinking about Gena and how neat she was. I thought about kissing her that night, holding her on the couch. She smelled so great. She was so warm. It seemed like we were the only ones in the room, even though the house was packed with kids.

And of course I thought about Mom and Dad. It felt strange knowing that they weren't downstairs in the den, reading or watching TV, or doing whatever they did after Cara and I went to bed. I didn't feel scared. It just felt strange.

I felt bad about the fight we had had in the morning. But that wasn't my fault, I told myself. Lying there, twisting this way and that in the dark, I got all worked up, having the argument all over again in my mind.

When I looked at the clock it said 1:42, almost two in the morning and I was still wide awake. I got out of bed and walked over to my bedroom window. I don't know why. Maybe I thought I'd see Mom and Dad's car in the drive.

I looked down over the front yard. The yellow porch light cast strange, shifting shadows over the lawn. It was very foggy. I could barely make out the streetlight across the street. Beyond it, the dark woods disappeared into gray-blue mist.

I pressed my forehead against the windowpane. The glass felt cool and soothing on my hot head. From somewhere in the woods I could hear two animals howling in unison. I listened carefully, even more wide awake now. The howls didn't sound like dog howls.

I looked out again. That gray van hadn't moved. It was still parked directly across the street.

The howls seemed to grow louder, closer. Suddenly I saw someone running across the lawn toward the street.

I blinked once, twice. I was only half-awake. I thought maybe my eyes were playing tricks on me.

No. It was Roger. I could see him clearly in the yellow porch light. His tan safari jacket flapped behind him in the wind as he ran. His long, thin shadow seemed to stretch back across the leaf-covered lawn.

He ran quickly in a straight line. As he crossed the street, the side door of the van slid open, and he disappeared into it, two hands helping to pull him up. Then the van door slid closed.

"What's going on?" My voice came out in a choked whisper.

I stared out into the fog. The van was dark and silent now. Shadows shifted on the front lawn. The surrounding darkness seemed to grow even darker.

I realized I was shivering and stepped back from the window.

What was going on? Why was Roger running out to that van in the middle of the night? Who was he meeting there?

Still shivering, I turned toward the door. I decided to wake Cara. But then something beside the bed caught my eye.

It was a soft white glow. Something was glowing on my bed table. I started toward it, stumbled, and stubbed my toe against the leg of my bed.

"Ow!" I hopped on one foot waiting for the pain to subside. Angrily, I made my way to the bed table, grabbed up the glowing object, and turned on the lamp.

It was the white monkey head.

Its rhinestone eyes glowed even brighter in the light. Its tight smile seemed to be grinning up at me, laughing at me.

Had I carried the monkey head into my room? I didn't remember putting it on my bed table. But I must have. I was so tired last night, I just didn't remember. . . .

I tossed it onto the bed and then walked back to the window. The van was still there across the street, dark and closed up. Roger was still inside.

Something very weird is going on here, I thought, now fully awake. I decided to run up to Roger's room while he was outside. Maybe I could find something up there, some clue as to what Roger was up to. He'd been acting strange all night. But running out to a van in the middle of the night was too strange to ignore.

As I pulled on my flannel robe, I struggled to come

up with a logical explanation. He's buying drugs, I thought.

No. Roger was a total straight-arrow. I'd never seen him drink more than half a beer in an evening. He wasn't into drugs.

Then what? A girlfriend?

Yes, that could be it. He could be meeting a girl.

But that didn't make sense, either. Why wouldn't he just invite her in? And I'd seen the van parked out there hours earlier. If he *was* meeting a girl out there, why would he keep her waiting for so long?

He had obviously waited to make sure that Cara and I had fallen asleep. Whatever he was doing, he didn't want us to know about it.

But what could that be?

I stepped out into the hallway and headed toward the attic stairs. The floor creaked and squeaked as I walked. I hesitated outside Cara's door. Should I wake her?

I decided not to. I was just going to slip up to Roger's room, have a quick look around, see if I could find anything helpful, and then hurry back into bed. Whatever I found could wait until morning. At least one of us was getting some sleep.

I was on the first step up to the attic when I heard Roger right behind me. "Hey, Mark, what are *you* doing up?"

chapter

7

I spun around. The hallway was lit by a small, dim night-light down by the floor across from Cara's room. But even in the dim light, I could see that Roger was sweating and his face was flushed.

"You scared me," I whispered.

"Sorry. I seem to be making a habit of it tonight." He didn't smile. "What are you doing up?"

"I . . . well . . . I just went to the bathroom," I replied, thinking quickly.

"The bathroom is that way," he said, pointing back down the hall.

"I know. I—" I didn't know *what* I was going to say next. "Hey, where were *you*?" I asked.

"I couldn't sleep," he said, wiping his forehead with his hand. "Too much studying, I guess. I took a walk to clear my head."

He was lying. He took a walk right into that gray van.

"It's so warm out," he added quickly. "I can't

believe this is November." Then he pushed past me and started up the attic steps.

"Well, good night," I whispered. I decided not to call him on his lie, not to tell him I'd seen him climb into the van. I was just too tired and too confused. I wanted to tell Cara what I'd seen and then decide what to do about Roger.

"Night," he called back. He hurried up the steps, eager to get away from me and my questions, I guess.

And I sure had a lot of questions now. But it was too late. The questions all swirled around in my head like clothes in a washing machine, heavy, heavy clothes.

Suddenly, I felt very heavy, too. I lumbered back to my room and fell onto my bed without bothering to take off my robe. When I finally fell asleep, I had strange, uncomfortable dreams.

In one dream, I was abandoned in an endless parking lot. There were gray cars as far as I could see in all directions. I was all alone in the center of the lot. I didn't know which direction I was supposed to go. I didn't know which car was mine. I didn't know where to look to find a way out.

I had been left there by somebody. I remembered that. I had been abandoned there. But what was I supposed to do next?

When the alarm went off at seven, I awoke feeling very out-of-sorts. My muscles all ached. My head felt heavy. I didn't remember any of my other dreams. I just remembered that they were unpleasant.

"Give me a break!" I shouted, not at anyone or anything in particular—just at the world in general.

I stretched and turned onto my side. I was startled

to see the white monkey head on my bed table beside the clock radio.

Again it seemed to be staring at me, grinning at me with that ugly, leering grin. The rhinestone eyes gleamed brightly even though there was little light in the room.

I picked it up and heaved it across the room. I heard it hit the wall and bounce across the carpet. "That'll teach you to stare," I said aloud.

Then, remembering Mom and Dad might be downstairs, I forced myself out of bed. I skipped my usual shower, pulled on yesterday's jeans and a striped pullover shirt that I thought was clean enough, and ran to the stairs.

Cara was right ahead of me. "Morning," I said.

She didn't reply. "Hey, Mom! Dad!" she called, as we both took the stairs two at a time. "Where *were* you two?"

We hurried into the kitchen. It was empty. Our dirty dishes from last night were still stacked on the counter beside the sink. "We didn't do a very good cleanup," Cara said.

"Who cares? Where are they?" I shouted.

"Don't yell at *me*. I don't know!"

"I wasn't yelling," I told her. Why was she trying to pick a fight?

"Maybe they're still asleep," she said, pushing past me. "I'll go up and see."

"I'll go with you." I don't know why I followed her. It certainly didn't take two of us to go look in their bedroom and see if they were back. I guess I just wasn't thinking clearly. I was feeling really worried, and when I start to worry, I go into high-gear worrying!

I stopped at the foot of the stairs and watched Cara run up to their room. A lot of horrible things flashed through my mind, horrible things that could've happened to Mom and Dad. "But if something horrible had happened," I argued with myself, "the police would've called by now." That thought made me feel a little better. But I knew I wouldn't feel a *lot* better until I knew where they were.

"Are they up there?" I shouted up the stairs to Cara.

She appeared above me at the top of the stairs. I noticed that her hair was unbrushed, which was really unusual for my sister. She shook her head dejectedly. "Nope. Not home."

My stomach growled. I suddenly realized I was starving. I wondered if there was anything in the house for breakfast. Then I felt bad thinking about food when I should've been worrying about Mom and Dad.

Cara slumped down the stairs and I followed her into the kitchen. We were both feeling pretty miserable. She found a box of cornflakes in the cabinet, but there was no milk. So we poured a bottle of Coke on it instead. "Every day should start with a balanced breakfast," Cara muttered.

Actually, it didn't taste that bad.

I had just about downed the entire bowl when I jumped up. I suddenly remembered the gray van.

"Hey! Where are you going?" Cara called after me as I ran to the living room and peered out the window. It was still dark out. The sun was just beginning to burn through the clouds. The van was gone.

"What are you doing, Mark?" Cara had followed me into the living room.

I motioned for her to sit down on the couch. Then I told her everything that had happened last night.

"And you definitely saw Roger run into this gray van?" she asked. "You're sure you weren't asleep?"

That's just like Cara. Always doubting everything.

"No, I wasn't asleep."

"And you're sure he didn't run past the van and it only looked like the van opened up because of shadows from trees or something?"

Now she was beginning to make me doubt what I'd seen with my own eyes. "No. I saw just what I said. Roger climbed into the van and the door closed."

"He definitely lied to you about taking a walk?"

"Cara, you're really starting to steam me!" I said, trying to control my temper.

"Okay, okay." She threw up her hands. "I'm sorry. It's just that if we're going upstairs to accuse Roger, we should be sure of what we're accusing him of."

"Well . . . it *was* dark on the street, and very foggy. But I'm sure I saw him climb in."

"Then let's go," Cara said, jumping off the couch and pulling me up. "We'll just put it to him—Roger, what were you doing in that gray van last night?"

"I guess." Cara had asked so many questions, I was beginning to think I'd dreamed the whole thing. Or maybe I was just reluctant to get into a big thing with Roger.

"Uh . . . Cara . . ." I said as we started up the stairs. "Maybe what Roger did last night isn't any of our business. He is entitled to a private life, after all."

Cara sighed and rolled her eyes. "Mark, our parents are missing, right?"

"Well . . . they didn't come home last night."

"And ever since they've been missing, Roger has been acting extremely weird. Wouldn't you agree?"

"Yeah, I guess."

"So we have every right to ask him why he's been acting so weird. Agreed?"

I thought about it for a short while. "Agreed." I had to give in. I never win any arguments with Cara unless I start shouting a lot. And this morning, I just didn't have the strength to shout.

Besides, she was right—for once.

We climbed the narrow stairs to the attic. It was about ten degrees warmer up here. Roger's door was closed.

"Should we wake him?" I whispered. "Or should we wait?"

Cara gave me a dirty look. "Of course we'll wake him. You *do* plan to go to school this morning, don't you?"

I knocked on the door softly, then harder.

No reply.

I had a sudden chill, a feeling of dread in the pit of my stomach. Something horrible has happened in there, I thought. I shook my head as if shaking away the thought. I knew I was just being stupid.

I knocked again. Still no reply.

So I pushed open the door and took a step inside.

Gray light filtered in through a small, dirt-smeared skylight. Roger's small cot was made, the thin green blanket tucked in tightly at all four corners. The room was empty. He had left already.

"I don't believe it," Cara said, disappointed that we wouldn't have our confrontation.

"He has morning classes," I said, moving toward the wall to make room for her.

"Not this early," Cara said, biting her lower lip. "Well . . . while we're here, let's take a look around."

"That won't take long," I said. I had to keep my head bent down so it wouldn't bump the ceiling.

I looked through a pile of stuff on Roger's desk, just a bunch of notebooks and texts. Cara got down on her hands and knees and looked under Roger's bed. "See anything?" I asked, whispering for some reason.

"Dust balls," she said, getting up quickly.

The bookshelf next to the desk was mostly empty, a few books and magazines tossed on the middle shelf. A cardboard cup containing marking pens and pencils was on the shelf below it.

"What a grim place," I said.

"Yeah. You'd think he'd put up some posters or something."

I looked at the bare gray walls. This was more like a prison cell than a college guy's room.

Cara started looking through the things on the top of the desk. "I already looked there," I said impatiently. I started to feel really nervous. I wanted to get out of there. What if Roger came back and found us snooping around in all his stuff?

"Hey! Look at this." Cara was holding up an empty notebook.

"A notebook. Big deal," I said.

"Right. An empty notebook." She picked up another one. "Look, Mark. This one is empty, too." I picked up the remaining notebook from the desk. Empty. Not a word written in it.

"So? What does that mean?" I asked. "He hasn't used these yet."

Cara was flipping through Roger's textbooks now. "Look. No underlining. Not a mark."

"So he doesn't like to mark up his books," I said, sighing. "I don't, either. I really don't think this is very interesting, Cara."

"But he hasn't taken a single note! None of this stuff looks like it's ever been opened!"

Suddenly I heard a creaking sound down in the hall. I glanced at Cara. She heard it, too.

We both froze. And listened.

Silence.

I peeked out the door. There was no one there. I tiptoed to the steps and looked down. No one. It was just the old house creaking.

When I got back to Roger's room, Cara was pulling out desk drawers and riffling through them. Since there was no dresser, Roger kept his clothes in the desk drawers. One entire drawer was filled with pairs of navy blue socks all neatly rolled into balls!

"Come on, Cara. Let's get out of here," I pleaded. "We're not going to find anything interesting. There's nothing here at all. It's as if Roger doesn't have a life."

She looked at me. "That's right. That's what's so weird. Don't you think that's interesting?"

"No," I said.

She pulled out the bottom desk drawer. It was filled nearly to the top with underwear. "Let's go," I said.

"We've found zip. Nada. Nothing." I started out the door.

"Wait, Mark! Oh, good Lord!"

I hurried back in. "Cara—what?"

She had pulled the underwear out of the drawer. Underneath it lay a shiny black snub-nosed pistol.

chapter

8

"*M*ark, what are you doing? Put that down!" I shouted. He had pulled the gun out of the drawer and was examining it.

"It's loaded," he said softly.

"Well, don't point it at me!"

"I'm not pointing it. I'm putting it back, okay?" he snapped.

"Just be careful."

He replaced the gun, handling it very gently. Then I shoved Roger's underwear back in on top of it and closed the desk drawer.

"Why do you think Roger keeps a loaded pistol in his room?" Mark asked, squinting his green eyes, thinking hard.

"Maybe he likes to shoot at cockroaches," I cracked.

He looked at me. He didn't seem to understand that I was joking. "Come on. Let's get out of here," I said, shoving him out the door.

Back in the kitchen, Mark started to pace. I sat down at the Formica counter. "Now what?" he asked.

I glanced up at the clock over the sink. It was seven-forty. If we didn't leave soon, we'd be late for school. "The phone," I said. "Maybe it's fixed."

We both raced to the wall phone. I got there first and grabbed the receiver. Silence. "Still dead," I sighed.

"We have to call the phone company," Mark said. "Mom and Dad have probably been trying to call all night."

"I know. I'll go down the block to Mrs. Fisher's house," I told him. I picked up my parents' little phone book. "Maybe her phone is working. I'll call Mom and Dad and then I'll call the phone company."

"I'd go with you, but Mrs. Fisher doesn't like me," Mark said. "She came over once when I was practicing my archery in the backyard, and ever since she's always giving me funny looks. She thinks I'm weird or something."

"She's right," I said, and quickly headed out the backdoor. I love getting the last word.

It was still chilly out. The sun hadn't managed to burn through the low, overhanging clouds. I should've put on a sweater or something, but Mrs. Fisher's house was just halfway down the block.

I walked quickly along the side of the street, past the nearly bare maple and sycamore trees. It was beginning to look like winter even though it didn't really feel that cold yet. When Mrs. Fisher's rambling old shingled house came into view, I picked up speed and jogged the rest of the way.

The front doorbell didn't seem to be working, so I

used the brass knocker in the center of the door. She came to the door after my second knock. A fairly attractive woman in her late forties or early fifties, she was wearing tan corduroy slacks and a plaid man's shirt. Her jet black hair was tied behind her head with a blue rubber band.

At first she stared at me. She looked very surprised to see me. "Cara?"

"Good morning, Mrs. Fisher. I'm sorry to bother you so early."

She held open the door so I could come in. "It's not early for me. I'm up at six every morning." The house smelled of coffee and stale cigarettes. "Is everything okay?"

She looked away when she asked that. Something about the way she asked it, with so much concern in her voice, made me suspicious. But of course I was being ridiculous. I think I'd suspect *anyone* this morning!

"Is your phone working? Ours is dead."

"Why, yes. It's working fine. I just spoke to my sister a few minutes ago. That's strange that yours is out."

"Yes," I agreed. "Can I use your phone?"

"Of course." I followed her through the living room, which was filled with heavy, dark antique furniture, into the kitchen, which wasn't much brighter.

"First I'm going to phone my parents," I said, searching the little directory for their direct number.

"Your parents?"

I looked up to see an odd expression on her face. It was more than surprise. It was shock. She saw me looking at her, and the expression quickly disappeared. She picked up a pack of cigarettes and forced one out of the pack. When she lit it, her hand was shaking.

"Yeah. They probably worked all night," I told her. Was I imagining that weird, shocked expression? I must have been. "They're not home."

With the cigarette dangling from her lips, Mrs. Fisher turned and walked over to the sink and started to rinse off some plates. "They didn't call you?"

"They couldn't. The phone's broken."

"Oh. Of course. Where do your parents work?" She didn't turn around. The dishes she was rinsing looked perfectly clean to me.

"At a place called Cranford Industries."

"Oh, yes. Cranford. They make airplane parts or something. I read about Cranford. They do a lot of work for the federal government, don't they?"

"I don't really know," I told her, picking up the phone receiver. "My parents install computer systems."

"Oh. That's interesting." She dried her hands and turned around. She put the cigarette down, then nervously picked it up again. "Cranford is pretty far away. At least two towns from here. Why did your parents buy a house here in Shadyside instead of nearer their work?"

"I don't know, Mrs. Fisher. I never really thought about it. I guess maybe they thought the high school was better here. You know. For Mark and me."

"Cara—" she started, but then she suddenly stopped.

"What?"

"Never mind," she said quickly. "I forgot what I

was going to say.'' She tossed the dish towel down on the counter. "I'd better hush up and let you make your calls.'' Looking nervous, she hurried out of the room, leaving the burning cigarette on an ashtray by the sink.

What's her problem? I asked myself. She'd always seemed so calm and normal whenever she came over to visit my parents. She was the only neighbor who was the least bit friendly. All of our other neighbors on Fear Street kept to themselves and never even waved or looked up when we went past.

I pushed my parents' direct line at Cranford Industries and then listened to the low ring. I let it ring six times, seven, eight. . . . No answer. The switchboard message center didn't pick up, either. It was too early, I guess. No one there yet.

I slumped against the counter, suddenly feeling sick. I was so disappointed. I really thought they'd be there.

Now what?

What could I do? Who could I call?

We had no relatives in Shadyside. We'd only been here since September. We hardly knew anyone!

What should I do? I couldn't go to school without knowing where Mom and Dad were, without knowing that they were okay. I couldn't sit there, class after class, wondering, just wondering what was going on.

I felt panicky and sick to my stomach. Maybe the cornflakes in Coca-Cola was a bad idea. My heart was pounding. I stared at the phone.

And suddenly I knew what Mark and I had to do. We had to go to Cranford Industries. We had to track my parents down.

But how? We could borrow a car. Or maybe rent

one. Or maybe there was a bus that went somewhere near there.

Yes. That's what we had to do. We had to cut school and go there. If Mom and Dad were there, we'd find out why we hadn't heard from them. And if they weren't there . . . well . . . They *had* to be there!

"Thank you, Mrs. Fisher!" I called.

There was no reply, so I ran out the door. I was halfway down the walk when I realized I'd forgotten to call the phone company about fixing our phone. So I hurried back into the house and called.

"No service at all?" a friendly woman on the other end asked, sounding truly concerned.

"No. It's totally silent," I told her.

"Strange. We haven't had any other complaints from your neighborhood," she said. "I'll notify the service guys right away."

"Thank you," I said and hung up, feeling a little better. I called my thanks up to Mrs. Fisher, who still hadn't reappeared, and hurried home, eager to tell Mark my idea about cutting school and going to Mom and Dad's office.

I ran up the drive and headed toward the backyard. But something caught my eye as I was about to pass the garage. Our garage doors have long, rectangular windows in them. And through the windows, I thought I saw something strange.

I stopped and walked up to the front door of the garage and peered in. Yes. I was right.

My parents' car—the blue Toyota they drove to work every day—it was there in the garage.

chapter
9

Mark opened the garage door and we stood in the drive gaping at the car as if we'd never seen one before. "How did Mom and Dad get to work?" Mark asked, stepping into the garage and looking into the car windows.

Of course there was another question that both of us were thinking but didn't dare say aloud: *Did* they get to work?

There was only one way to find out.

"We've got to go to Cranford—right now," I said.

Mark kicked a rear tire. "I can't, Cara. I've got a math test this morning. And I wanted to see Gena and—"

He stopped and made a face. He knew those things weren't as important as finding Mom and Dad.

"Oh, I don't know *what* to do!" he cried angrily and slammed his hand against the trunk. He looked just like a little boy having a tantrum. "Ow!" He'd hurt his hand.

"Stop kicking and slamming things," I said. "You're upset. I'm upset. The only way we're going to be less upset is to take some action."

"Okay, okay," he grumbled. "Lay off the lectures, okay? Let's get the car keys and our coats and get going. At least we have a car to drive."

We both looked at the car again. I felt weak. I turned away. That car shouldn't have been there. Something was wrong. Something was seriously wrong.

"Maybe they got a lift to work," Mark said as we hurried into the house to get our coats. "Maybe there was an emergency at Cranford, and someone came to pick them up."

"Maybe," I said. Neither of us believed it, though.

But what *could* we believe?

I grabbed my down coat, the extra set of car keys, and a road map from the desk in the den, and a few seconds later, Mark backed down the drive. The sun had given up its attempts to break through the clouds. It was gray and very windy. November was starting to look like November.

At the end of the block, Mark slammed on the brakes. "The van!" he cried.

The unmarked gray van he had told me about was parked in front of us. A man with very short, white-blond hair sat in the driver's seat.

Mark pulled the Toyota right up to the van. The blond man stared straight ahead, pretending not to notice us.

Mark unrolled his window and stuck his head out. "Hey! You waiting for Roger?" he yelled to the guy.

The guy in the van rolled down his window. "Sorry.

I had the radio cranked up. What did you want?" He flashed us a wide smile. He had rows and rows of perfect white teeth. I guess he was handsome. But with his white-blond hair, pale skin, and sparkling white teeth, he was practically an albino!

"You waiting for Roger?" Mark repeated.

"Who?"

"Roger."

The guy in the van shook his head. His smile hadn't faded an inch. "Sorry. You've got the wrong guy. I don't know any Roger."

Mark stared back at him, disappointed. "Oh. Sorry."

"No problem," the guy said, and rolled up his window.

Mark floored the gas pedal and we took off with a roar. "He's lying," Mark said.

"How do you know?" I asked.

"From his smile."

We both laughed. It wasn't really funny. We just needed to laugh. Then we both got very silent.

We had the car heater turned way up, but I felt really cold. I guess it was partly because I was so nervous, so worried about what they might tell us at Cranford Industries about our parents.

Mark drove with one hand. He stared straight ahead, driving like a robot or something.

Finally I couldn't stand the silence any longer. "What's the worst thing they could tell us?" I asked.

He didn't react. I couldn't tell if he was thinking about his answer or if he hadn't heard me.

"The worst thing?" he repeated finally, turning onto Division Street. "I guess the worst thing would be if they said, 'Your parents left work at the normal time last Tuesday. We've been wondering where they are, too. Why didn't they come in to work yesterday morning?' "

I didn't have to think about it. Mark was right. That *was* the worst thing they could say. "And what's the best thing they could say?" I asked, just making stupid conversation.

"That's easy," Mark said. "The best thing they could say is, 'Here come your parents now. Guess they've been really tied up here.' "

"Well . . . I suppose that's still a possibility," I said. But I didn't really believe it.

I knew our parents weren't just going to pop up at the office and apologize for not calling. But I hoped that maybe someone there would have some kind of logical explanation for us.

But what would be a logical explanation?

I tried not to think. I tried not to think of all the horrible things that could have happened to them. But of course there was no way to shut those thoughts out. The worst thoughts, the ugliest, most terrifying thoughts always find you, always work their way into your brain.

We found the entrance to the industrial park and followed the sign to Cranford Industries. It was an enormous three-story white building, not as modern as I'd imagined, surrounded by a beautifully manicured lawn dotted with evergreen trees. We weren't sure where to park, and there wasn't anyone around to help us. Finally, we found a large lot in the back of the building. As we pulled up to it, an armed guard stepped out from a small booth beside the drive and motioned for us to stop.

"Pass," he said, reaching out his hand to Mark.

"Huh? You're letting us pass?"

"Pass," the guard repeated, a little more insistent.

"Oh! Uh . . . we don't have a pass. We're visitors."

The guard held up a long pad and glanced down a list. "Names?"

"We're not on your list," I said. "We don't have an appointment. We came to see our parents."

"Their names?" He flicked through the pad until he came to another, longer list.

"Burroughs. Lucy and Greg Burroughs," Mark said.

"Not on my list," the guard said, eyeing us suspiciously.

"They're pretty new," I said weakly.

He leaned down and peered into the car, looking Mark and me up and down. Then he looked into the backseat. "Well . . . park in Twenty-three-B over there. Then go around to the front. They'll check you out inside."

"Thank you," Mark and I both said gratefully. I felt as if I'd passed some important test. But why should it be such a big deal to let two teenagers park so they can see their parents?

Anyway, we parked in 23-B and walked around to the front entrance, just as the guard had ordered. "Hey, wait up!" I yelled. Mark was practically running.

"Sorry." He stopped and waited for me to catch up. "This place is pretty impressive," he said.

"It's so big," I said, pushing open one of the glass

doors of the front entrance. "How does anyone find anyone here?"

Another guard, this one very young, with cold blue eyes and a blond stubble under his nose that was trying to become a mustache, came up to meet us the instant we entered.

"You're the visitors?" he asked, looking us up and down the way the parking-lot guard had.

"Yes," we both managed to say.

"Burroughs," he said. The other guard had talked to him by phone or radio already. "Hold still. This won't hurt a bit."

He had a metal detector in his hand, the kind they have at airports, and he moved it over Mark and then me, checking us out from head to foot.

Mark and I looked at each other. I think we were both thinking, What kind of crazy place to work at was this!

"Okay," the guard said. "Follow me."

He led us through the large, open lobby. It appeared to go the entire length of the building. It looked very plush. There were leather couches and chairs in small clusters all around. There were large oil paintings on all the walls. A polished brass staircase wound up to the top floors from the center of the enormous lobby. Our sneakers squeaked over the marble floor as we tried to keep up with the guard, who was walking really fast.

I glanced at Mark. He looked as nervous as I felt.

Finally, after walking for what seemed like miles, we came to a young woman seated behind a long, wooden desk set diagonally near the foot of the stair-case. The guard left us there without a word and returned to his post by the door. We waited for her to look up from her notebook, a logbook of some kind which she was staring into. She was very pretty, I noticed. She had her straw-blond hair pulled back tight, and she was wearing a great-looking plum-colored suit with matching tie.

Finally, she put down her notebook and flashed us an automatic smile. "Can I help you?"

"Uh . . . we came to see our parents," Mark blurted out.

"Do they work here?"

Before we could answer, the desk phone buzzed and she picked it up. She talked for three or four minutes, looking up at us from time to time. The longer we waited, the more nervous I felt. I had pains in my stomach and I was starting to feel a little light-headed.

Finally, she put down the phone. But it rang again, and again she had a three- or four-minute conversation while Mark and I stood there, trying to keep it together.

I stared at everyone who passed by. They were mostly people in business suits, heading for the staircase, their well-polished shoes clicking loudly over the marble floor. I kept thinking maybe Mom and Dad would just show up.

And then I saw them.

They were walking quickly toward us from the far end of the lobby, walking arm in arm.

"Mom! Dad!" I cried. "Hi!"

Mark and I started running toward them. They didn't seem to see us.

"Hey! Hi, you two!" I cried happily.

But as we got closer, I realized it wasn't them.

Mark and I stopped running. The man and woman looked a little like Mom and Dad, but not that much, really. I think my imagination was working overtime.

They walked right past us and headed up the stairway.

Mark and I avoided looking at each other. I guess he felt as foolish as I did. "Sorry," I said.

He didn't say anything. We walked back to the receptionist and waited for her to get off the phone.

"Now, who did you wish to see?" she asked after a few more endless minutes had passed.

"Our parents," I said. "The name is Burroughs. Lucy and Greg Burroughs."

She pushed a few keys on her desk computer and then stared at the screen. "Hmmm . . . How do you spell Burroughs?"

I spelled it for her and she typed a few words on the keyboard. A list of names appeared on the green monitor screen, and she slowly ran her finger down them. After a few seconds she looked up, her finger still on the screen. "Sorry. No Burroughs listed here."

"But that's impossible," Mark said. He suddenly looked angry.

"Know what? I'll bet you're in the wrong building," the receptionist said.

"Wrong building?" Marked turned and looked back toward the entrance at the end of the lobby.

"This is Cranford Industries," the receptionist said. "There are a lot of buildings in this industrial park. You probably want—"

"Cranford Industries," Mark insisted. "That's right. This is where our parents work."

"They just started in September," I told her. "Maybe they aren't in the computer yet."

"Well . . ." She thought about it for a while. "The computer listing is updated every week. Tell me, do you know what division they work in?"

"Computers," I said. "They install mainframe computers."

"Computers?" She frowned. "Tell you what. Let me talk to Mr. Blumenthal. He's the personnel director."

"Thank you," Mark and I said at the same time.

I felt very confused. Why weren't Mom and Dad in the directory?

As I watched the receptionist phone Mr. Blumenthal, I answered my own question. It was quite simple. Mom and Dad weren't regular employees of Cranford Industries. They were special project workers. They were here to install mainframe computers. They weren't really part of any division. So of course they weren't listed in the company directory.

These thoughts made me feel a little better. But I was still terribly nervous, and the endless shuffle of people across the large lobby, the clicking shoes on the marble, the bright lights were all making me feel very uncomfortable.

She turned away as she talked to Mr. Blumenthal, and I couldn't hear what she was saying. A few seconds later, she hung up and, looking very concerned, punched another phone number. "Mr. Blumenthal told me to call. Is Mr. Marcus available?" I heard her say.

Who was Mr. Marcus?

She turned away again and I couldn't hear the rest

of her conversation. Finally she put down the phone and turned back to us. "Mr. Marcus will see you in a few minutes."

"Is he in personnel?" I asked.

"He's our CEO," she said, looking at me as if I'd just barfed all over her desk. I guess I was supposed to know who Mr. Marcus was.

"CEO?" Mark asked.

"Chief executive officer," the receptionist said, frowning at Mark's ignorance. "Why don't you have a seat?" She pointed to two enormous leather chairs across from her desk. Then she took another call.

Mark and I walked over to the chairs, but we didn't sit down. We were too nervous, too eager to get this over with.

"Why is the big boss going to see us?" Mark whispered.

I shrugged. His guess was as good as mine.

A few minutes later, a young woman came down the staircase. She was carrying a stack of files. She told us she was Mr. Marcus's secretary and led us up the stairs, down several long hallways of offices and cubicles, and finally into Mr. Blumenthal's gigantic corner office.

Mr. Marcus smiled at us and put down the phone. He was a young man with short brown hair slicked straight back. He wore heavy black-framed glasses. "Hi. Nice to meet you. No school today?" he said, speaking quickly. He motioned for us to sit down in the two chairs in front of his desk.

"We skipped school," Mark said abruptly, looking very uncomfortable.

Mr. Marcus laughed. But he stopped when he saw the serious looks on our faces.

"We want to see our parents. We have a problem," I added.

"Well, I'll get them for you right away," he said. "I can see you kids are upset. Emergency at home?"

"No. Not really," I said. "We just need to see them."

"I'll get them for you right away. Even sooner," he said, giving us a warm smile. I liked him immediately. I could see how he got to be the big cheese at such a young age. He seemed so . . . trustworthy, so dependable. He seemed like a real person.

"Who are your parents?" he asked.

"Burroughs. Lucy and Greg Burroughs," I told him.

He took off his heavy eyeglasses and rubbed the bridge of his nose. Quickly replacing them, he punched some keys on the computer next to his desk. "Burroughs . . . Burroughs . . ."

"They just started in September," I said, my voice shaking. "They came here to install mainframe computers."

He looked away from the computer screen. "Computers?"

"Yes. They install computers. They—"

"We're not having any computers installed," he said, suddenly looking very confused. He stared first at Mark, then at me.

"You're not?"

"No. I don't have anyone here installing new computers."

"But our parents—"

He stood up. He was much taller than I'd thought. "Are you sure you kids have the right company?"

"Yes," I said. I was getting tired of that question.

"Well, I'm really sorry," Mr. Marcus said. "But I don't see how I can help you." He studied the computer screen for a moment. He pushed a few more keys and studied it some more.

"Nope," he said finally. "There's no one named Burroughs working here. There never has been."

chapter

10

"*I* felt like I was in a dream or something," I said. "Like nothing was real. Everything was all topsy-turvy."

Cara nodded. "I know. I felt the same way. I don't think I'll ever forget the look on Marcus's face. He felt so bad for us."

"Yeah. I know. And what he said just keeps repeating in my mind. 'There's no one named Burroughs working here. There never has been.' "

Cara and I were sitting in Shadyside Park, the large park that stretches behind the high school and ends at the Conononka River on the edge of town. The park was bleak and empty. The trees were bare. Everything was gray.

I was sitting on a low tree stump. Cara was sitting with her legs crossed on the hard ground, her down jacket zipped up to her chin, her blond hair fluttering in the gusting wind.

We hadn't said anything to each other all the way

back from Cranford Industries. I think we were both in total shock.

It was just a little hard to accept the fact that our parents had lied to us, that they didn't work where they said they worked. And that now we had no way to get in touch with them at all.

At first we hadn't believed Mr. Marcus. We were sure he had to be mistaken. But he checked the computer three times. And he called the personnel department to make sure there hadn't been a computer error.

But no. What he had told us was correct. *There's no one named Burroughs working here. There never has been.*

Marcus had offered to help us. He really was very sympathetic. He saw how destroyed Cara and I were. But what could he do?

We practically ran out of the building. We just wanted to get away from there. The parking-lot guard tried to stop us at the exit, but I just bombed right past him and drove away.

And now we sat in the cold park, looking up at the back of the high school, trying to figure out what to do next. Across the grass, two robins pecked at the cold, hard ground. They didn't seem to be having much luck finding lunch. Things were tough all over.

"So what are we going to do?" I asked.

Cara shook her head. "Call the police, I guess."

"I guess."

"Why did they lie to us?" Cara cried, suddenly sounding very emotional.

"I don't know. I haven't a clue. I just don't get it, Cara." I stared at the robins. I didn't want to look at her. I didn't want to get too emotional. I wanted to stay as calm as possible, but I could feel myself starting to lose it.

"Let's think," she said, uncrossing her legs. "Let's try to put together everything we know."

"What for?" I asked gloomily.

"Because maybe we'll think of something. Maybe we can figure it all out."

"Yeah. Sure." What was there to figure out? Our parents lied to us and then they left.

No. That was impossible. I told myself to stop thinking like that. "Okay. Let's put together the pieces," I said.

"What day is it?" Cara asked.

"Oh. You're in great shape," I muttered sarcastically. "It's Wednesday."

"Okay. So yesterday was Tuesday. Mom and Dad left for work in the morning."

"Only we don't know if they left for work because the car was still in the garage," I reminded her. "And we don't know where they work—or even if they *do* work!" I cried, jumping up and walking around in a circle.

"Okay, okay. Try to stay calm." She motioned for me to sit back down, but I didn't feel like it.

"Let's concentrate on what we know," Cara said, leaning back, supporting herself with her hands on the ground. "We know they didn't come home last night."

"Duh."

"Stop being so sarcastic. You always think getting angry and moody is going to solve things. But it never does."

She was right. I apologized.

"Then we found that white monkey head in their bed," she continued. "That's some kind of clue, don't you think?"

"I guess. And don't forget we caught Roger snooping around in Mom and Dad's room."

"He was at the window. What could he have been doing at the window?" she asked.

We both thought hard.

"I know. He could have been signaling to the guy in the van," I said.

Cara nodded. "Maybe. You could be right. And what do we know about the van?"

"Nothing," I said.

"Just that it was parked across from our house most of the night. And you saw Roger sneak out and get into the van."

"That guy in the van with the platinum hair said he didn't know Roger," I said.

"He had to be lying," Cara said. "And don't forget we found a gun hidden in Roger's room. That's a clue, too."

"So we have some clues. But what help are they?" I asked impatiently.

"Will you stop whining?"

"I'm not whining. Get off my case."

"We have to talk to Roger," Cara said, "before we call the police. He *is* our cousin, after all. Maybe he's in some kind of trouble."

"Okay," I agreed. "We'll talk to Roger. Then we'll call the police."

We turned toward the school and saw kids hurrying out of the building. "It must be lunchtime," I said.

"We can go in now and try to call Roger on the pay phone."

We got to the door to the school just as Cory Brooks and his pal David Metcalfe were coming out.

"Hey—you guys sleep in today?" Cory asked, grinning.

"Great party last night," Metcalfe said. "We gonna do it again tonight?"

"Looks like they had *too much* partying," Cory said. "Look at 'em!"

He and Metcalfe laughed. "Later," Metcalfe said, and they headed toward the student parking lot.

"Funny guys," I muttered.

We walked through the crowded, noisy corridors to the pay phone by the principal's office. A girl was using it and we had to wait.

"Maybe Mom and Dad are home," Cara said. "Maybe Mom will pick up the phone."

"Maybe fish can talk," I said. She shoved me. I fell into the phone booth, and the girl inside gave me a dirty look.

A few minutes later she came out and I stepped in. I dropped in my quarter and pushed our home number. The phone rang once. Twice. "It's ringing," I told Cara.

"What?" It was so noisy in the hallway, she couldn't hear me.

I didn't know whether the phones at home were fixed or not. Sometimes phones ring normally even though they're out of order. I let it ring eight times. I was about to hang up when I heard a click. Someone had picked up.

"Hello?"

I recognized the voice at once. "Roger?"

"Yeah. Mark? Where are you?"

"In school. The phones are fixed?"

"Yeah. I guess so. We're talking to each other, so they must be fixed."

"That's great. Listen, are my mom and dad home?"

His voice dropped. "No. Not yet."

"No word from them or anything?"

"No."

"Listen, Roger, we've got to talk. I want to ask you—"

"I've got to run, Mark. I was just on my way out the door. We'll talk later, okay?"

"Okay, but—"

"You and Cara are all right?"

"Yeah, sure, we're fine. But—"

"Good. Talk to you later. Don't worry." And he hung up.

"Well, at least the phones are fixed," I told Cara.

"Let's go get lunch," she said. "I'm starving."

When we got to the lunchroom, Cara wandered off to have lunch with Lisa and Shannon. I looked for Gena, but she wasn't there. She wasn't at our usual meeting place across from the gym, either. And she wasn't in our fifth-period government class, so I figured she must have stayed home.

I hoped she wasn't sick. I really wanted to talk to her.

I daydreamed about her the rest of the afternoon. I guess I was trying to avoid thinking about Mom and Dad. I didn't stop thinking about her. I kept trying to relive last night on the couch, trying to remember how she felt, how she *tasted*. I wondered if I was in love or something. She was such a fox! There were girls I'd daydreamed about at my other schools, but not like this.

I called her as soon as I got home—well, right after checking to see if Mom and Dad were back. They weren't. And Roger wasn't home, either.

I was feeling really down. I planned to go out in the backyard and fire off a whole quiver of arrows after I talked to Gena.

The phone rang and rang. Finally, Gena answered. I could tell by the sound of her voice as she said hello that something was wrong. Her voice was shaky, as if she'd been crying.

"Hi, Gena? It's me. Where were you today? Are you okay?"

And then she started to talk and cry at the same time. She sounded very strange; upset but frightened, too. I had trouble understanding her at first. I guess I didn't *want* to understand her because of what she was saying.

"I don't *believe* this," I said, my heart pounding. I suddenly had a throbbing pain at both temples. "But, come on, Gena—you don't—you're not serious! But why? I mean—I don't *believe* you! *Why are you doing this?*"

chapter

11

I got home about five o'clock. The house was dark. No one seemed to be home.

What a rotten day. It had to be the worst day of my life, and finding the house dark and empty didn't help to lift my spirits any.

If only Mom and Dad would get back. I just felt so strange not talking to them for two whole days. I let out a little cry as the thought flashed through my mind that I might never talk to them again.

Where was Mark, anyway?

I dropped my book bag on the kitchen counter and checked the refrigerator for a message. Nothing. Feeling totally worn out and miserable, I slumped into the living room.

"*Hey!*"

Someone was sitting in the dark on the couch.

"Only me." It was Mark. He didn't move or look up.

"You scared me to death," I said, feeling my heart pound. "Why are you sitting in the dark?"

He didn't answer.

"What's wrong? What are you doing, Mark?"

Still no reply.

My first thought was that he had gotten bad news about Mom and Dad.

I flicked the light switch. The lamp by the front window lit up. Mark turned away so I couldn't see his face.

"What *is* it?" I screamed. "Is it Mom and Dad? Are they—"

"No," he said, without turning around.

"Have you heard from them?"

"No."

I felt really relieved. I walked over to the couch and stood in front of him.

"Get out of my face," he said, looking down. "Take a walk."

"Mark, what is your problem?"

He took a deep breath and slowly let it out. He looked up at me. I think he'd been crying. I wasn't sure. I don't think I'd seen him cry since he was eight or nine. But his face looked puffy and his eyes were red.

"Are you okay?" I sat down at the other end of the couch.

"Take a walk," he muttered.

"Come on."

He shook his head. "Okay. If I tell you, will you leave me alone? Gena broke up with me."

I wasn't sure I heard right. "She *what?*"

"She broke up with me. Do you understand English? She doesn't want to see me again."

The scene on this same couch the night before

flashed into my mind. I saw Gena sitting on Mark's lap. I saw them making out despite the room full of people.

I stared at Mark in disbelief and he turned away again. "Don't look at me like that."

"I'm sorry," I said. I really was. "I don't know what to say."

"Well, don't say anything." Whenever he was upset about something, Mark got angry at the nearest person. I decided if it would make him feel better to yell at me, then let him.

"When did she tell you?"

"I called right after school. She wasn't in school today."

"And she said—"

"She sounded weird. Scared, sort of. I don't know. She didn't sound like herself."

"She said she wanted to break up?"

"She said she couldn't see me anymore."

"Couldn't, or didn't want to?"

He scowled. "Give me a break."

"Well, it's an important difference," I said. "Did she give a reason?"

"No. No reason. Just said not to call her anymore or try to talk to her in school or anything."

"Weird. So what did you say?"

"I went over to her house."

"You did? Just now?"

"Yeah. Right after she told me."

"And what did she say?"

Mark got up quickly and walked to the window. He stood staring out into the graying night, his back to me. "I didn't see her. Her father answered the door."

"And?"

"He was very nice about it. He just said that Gena was very upset, so upset she stayed home from school. I told him I just wanted to talk to her. But he said she didn't want to talk to me."

"So what did you do?"

Mark spun around angrily and scowled at me. "So what *could* I do? I turned around and came home, of course. Then you arrived and started giving me the third degree."

"I did not. I just asked why you were sitting like a statue in a dark room."

"Well, now you know," he said bitterly.

I should've dropped it, but knowing when to shut up isn't one of my better talents. "But it doesn't make any sense. Gena really seemed to like you. I mean, last night—"

"Shut up about last night!" he flared.

"Sorry. I just meant that you two didn't have any kind of fight or disagreement or anything."

"No. Nothing," he agreed, pacing the length of the room. "I've only known her three weeks. We didn't have *time* to fight about anything."

"So why in heaven's name—"

"I don't know. It's a mystery."

"But you and she—"

"I don't want to talk about it anymore." He started pacing faster.

"Mark, I think we should call the police right now," I said.

He stopped pacing and turned around to face me. It was pitch-black outside the window now. Darkness came so early in November. The lamp by the window wasn't bright enough. The dim light it cast over the old furniture just made the room more gloomy. I suddenly felt chilled.

"Yeah, I guess you're right. Sorry I barked at you like that, Cara. I just felt like—like my whole life is crumbling, you know?"

"Yes, I know," I said quietly.

We walked into the kitchen to call the police. I turned on every light we passed. The house was just too creepy in the dark.

"Let me do it," Mark said, picking up the receiver. "Should we just dial nine-one-one?"

"I guess—no, wait." I suddenly remembered the policeman who had come to the door the night before and the card he had given me. Now, where had I put it? I reached into my jeans pocket and found it crumpled up in there.

"What's that?" Mark asked suspiciously.

"That policeman who was here—Captain Farraday. This card has his direct line."

"Good. Maybe you should call." Mark backed away from the phone. I wondered if I looked as worried and upset as he did.

"Are you okay?" I asked. His broad forehead was covered with little drops of perspiration.

"No," he said, frowning. "Why should I be okay?"

I held the little card in one hand and pushed the numbers with the other. He picked up after the first ring. "Police. Farraday speaking."

"Oh. Captain Farraday. Hi."

"Yes. Who's this?" he asked brusquely.

"It's Cara Burroughs. Remember me?"

"Sure, Cara. Of course I remember you. That party isn't still going on, is it?"

"No. I'm . . . uh . . . calling about my parents."

His voice turned serious. "Yes. What about them?"

"Well . . ." I suddenly felt very strange, as if this wasn't really happening. I wasn't really calling the police to report my parents missing, was I? That didn't happen in real life.

"My parents didn't come home last night and they aren't home now."

There was a long silence. "That's strange," he said finally, his voice quieter, sympathetic. "Did they call or anything?"

"No. The phone was broken for a while. But my brother and I haven't heard a word from them."

"I'm writing this down, Cara," he said. "I don't think there's anything to worry about, but I'm getting it down. Have they ever done this before? You know, not come home?"

"A couple of times. Especially when they were starting new jobs. But they always called."

"I see." There was silence while he wrote. "Did you call their office?"

"Well, that's sort of a problem," I said. I told him quickly about our trip this morning to Cranford Industries and what Mr. Marcus had told us.

"This is very strange, isn't it," Farraday said. I could tell he was taking notes. "But I'm sure we can clear it up really fast." His voice was calm and reassuring. I wished I had called him sooner.

"Let me look through some things here," Farraday said. I could hear him shuffling through papers. "I don't have any accident reports." More shuffling. "No serious crime reports, either. So you don't have to think the worst. Nothing terrible has happened to them.''

"That's a relief," I said.

Mark grabbed my shoulder. "Does he know where they are?"

I waved him away and shook my head no. "They weren't in an accident or anything," I whispered to Mark.

"I know how it is," Farraday said, still rustling papers. "You start imagining the most horrible things, right?"

"Yeah, I guess," I said. "Do you think we should—"

"Tell you what," he interrupted. I could hear a police radio start to blare in the background. "I'll get some men on this right away. Maybe I'll even send one out to Cranford just to make sure there wasn't some kind of mistake."

"Oh, thank you," I said.

"Shadyside is a pretty small town," Farraday said. "I think we'll locate your parents very soon."

"Will you call me back?" I asked.

"Right. I'll either call or send a patrolman by."

"Thanks, Captain. I really feel better already."

"Well, don't get crazy worrying, you hear? When I catch up with your parents, I'm gonna give 'em a good talking to, tell them they shouldn't be neglecting such good kids."

"Okay, I—"

"But the main thing is not to worry. If something bad had happened, I would've received a report by now."

"Thanks again," I said. " 'Bye."

I was about to hang up the receiver when I heard a loud click. I realized immediately what it was.

Roger was upstairs. And he'd been listening in on the attic extension.

I felt a sudden chill. Why didn't he just come downstairs if he wanted to know what was going on?

Why was Roger *spying* on us?

chapter

12

"*R*oger was spying on us," Cara said, hanging up the phone.

"Huh?"

"You heard me. He was listening in on the upstairs extension."

"Are you sure?"

She didn't answer me. She went running to the front steps. "Hey, Roger! Roger!"

I followed her and heard Roger coming down the attic steps. "Yeah?"

"Why were you spying on us, Roger?" Cara wasn't exactly being subtle.

Roger appeared on the second-floor landing. He looked tired. The front of his sweatshirt had dark stains on it. His usually perfectly slicked-back hair was heading in all directions.

"Hi, Cara. What did you say? I just got home. I was upstairs."

"I know you were upstairs. You were upstairs listening in on my phone conversation," Cara said angrily, glaring up at him.

Roger's eyes bulged in surprise. He ran a hand back through his hair. "What? No. I went up to get changed. I spilled stuff on my sweatshirt and—"

"I heard the click, Roger." Cara wasn't going to let him off the hook. I agreed with her. Roger had been acting too suspicious ever since Mom and Dad disappeared. It was time to confront him.

"Phones click for a lot of reasons," Roger said, not making any move to come down to us. "I wasn't listening in, Cara. I'd never do that."

"Roger, there are some questions Mark and I need to ask you," Cara started.

But Roger interrupted. "Cara, who were you talking to—your mom and dad?"

"No. You know it wasn't," Cara insisted.

"I really wasn't listening in," Roger said, leaning against the banister. "You have no reason to suspect me."

"Yes, we do," I broke in. "I saw you run out last night."

"You mean real late? Right. I told you when I came in. I couldn't sleep. I went for a walk."

"But I saw the van, Roger. I saw you climb into it."

He looked surprised. "Climb into a van? Me? Are you sure, Mark? Are you sure it was me?"

"Well, of course. Who else?" He was starting to get me steamed.

"Are you sure you were fully awake? When I went out for my walk, I did see a van parked outside. But why would I climb into it?"

"That's what we want to know," Cara said angrily.

"And why do you have a gun in your room?" I added.

"Huh?" His mouth dropped open. "A gun?"

"In your bottom desk drawer."

He dropped down onto the top stair. "You searched my room?"

"Well, yes," I said. "But we—"

"You searched my room, and then you accuse *me* of spying?" He sounded really hurt and upset.

"Roger, we—" Cara started.

"Who gave you the right to go through my things?"

"Nobody," I said. "It's just that you've been acting weird lately, so we thought we'd look around."

"I haven't been acting weird. You two have," Roger said, shaking his head. "Of course I can understand why. You're upset about your parents. But sneaking into my room, making crazy accusations, and hallucinating people climbing into vans isn't going to help get your parents back."

"We didn't hallucinate the pistol," I said. "We saw it."

"Yes, I have a pistol," Roger said. "It so happens that that pistol means a lot to me."

"What do you mean?" I asked.

"It belonged to my dad. He was a policeman. He gave it to me on my eighteenth birthday. He told me I should always keep it nearby. He said he hoped I never had to use it, but he wanted me to have it anyway. A few weeks later, he was shot dead in a drug raid." Roger turned away. "That pistol is about the only thing I have left from my dad."

"Look, Roger, I'm sorry that we went in your room," I said.

"Me, too," Cara said quietly.

"No need to apologize," Roger said, climbing to his feet. "It's just that we've got to stick together now. We've got to trust each other. Know what I mean?"

"Yeah," I said.

"We can't panic and start turning on each other. We have to—"

"I called the police," Cara said, interrupting.

"Very good idea," Roger said. "We should've done it sooner." He glanced at his watch. "Oh, I'm late. I've got to run. I'll be back later and we can talk. Okay?"

Cara didn't say anything. She just turned and headed back toward the kitchen.

"Yeah. Later," I said, and gave Roger a little wave. Then I followed Cara.

"He's a very bad liar," Cara whispered after we heard him climb the attic stairs.

"How do you know he's lying?" I asked. "He seems like such a nice guy," I said.

"You think *everyone* is a nice guy," Cara cracked. "But I don't believe his story about the gun. It was just too cornball for words. Also, if he just keeps it as a memento, why was the gun loaded?"

"Cara!" She was always so cynical. I was sure Roger was telling the truth. He looked so sad, thinking about his father.

"Hey, we've got to get some dinner. Is there any food in this house?" Cara asked.

We began to search the kitchen for something to eat. I found a loaf of white bread in the bread drawer that was only a little stale. Cara found a jar of peanut butter on the top shelf of the food cabinet.

She opened the lid and looked inside. "Just enough for two sandwiches if we spread it pretty thin."

"What a feast," I said sarcastically. "At least is there some jelly?"

Cara opened the refrigerator and found a jar of grape jelly. She said something to me, but I didn't hear her. I was thinking about Gena. I kept hearing her voice again and again, hearing her words again as she told me we couldn't see each other again.

What had happened? Why did she do it?

"You didn't hear a word I said." Cara's voice broke into my thoughts.

"You're right," I said glumly.

"Poor Mark," she said. I looked up to see if she was being sarcastic, but she wasn't.

"It's like I've lost everyone at once," I said.

"Don't say that," Cara snapped. "Nobody is lost forever. Stop thinking like that. Just eat your peanut-butter sandwich. You'll feel better if you eat something."

"You sound just like Mom," I told her.

We both sort of stared at each other, then picked up our sandwiches. Peanut butter is such a bad idea when you're upset and not terribly hungry. It sticks to your mouth and teeth, and it takes so much effort to chew. Neither of us was in a mood to work so hard—for so little reward. We sat there glumly, not talking, not looking at each other.

I had only taken a couple of bites when I heard Roger run down the front stairs and then heard the door close behind him. Cara jumped up. "Let's follow him."

"What?"

"Let's follow him. I want to know where he's going."

"No," I said, trying to pull her back into her chair. "That's a bad idea."

"If you won't come, I'll go alone," she said. She pulled out of my grasp and ran toward the front hall.

"But someone has to stay here for when the police call," I said.

"What that means is you want to call Gena," she said, pulling on her down jacket.

"Well, that, too," I admitted. "But I really don't see the point of—"

" 'Bye." And she was out the door.

"What a wild-goose chase," I said aloud to the empty room. Roger was probably going off to a friend's place to study. I figured that Roger had made some friends at college. He'd never mentioned any or brought anyone home with him. And he never talked on the phone that much. But he must have had some friends, at least some people he liked to study with.

Why did Cara decide to play detective? I guess it was better than sitting around this creepy old house waiting for the phone to ring.

Just as I had that thought, the phone rang.

"Hello," I said, expecting to hear the police captain Cara had spoken to.

"Mark? It's me. I—"

It took me a while to recognize Gena's voice. She sounded terribly frightened.

"Gena? What's going on?"

"I can't talk now. I have to tell you . . . It's very important that—you have to—"

"Gena? Gena?"

It sounded like some kind of struggle. I thought I heard her cry out.

Then I heard a click.

"Gena? Gena? Are you still there?" I cried.

The dial tone buzzed in my ear.

chapter

13

*T*he most direct way to Gena's house was through the Fear Street woods. Sure, the kids at school had told me all these scary stories about the Fear Street woods. But I didn't care. I had to get there as fast as possible.

I put on my down jacket and pulled a flashlight off the shelf in the front closet. I knew that if I went straight through the woods behind our house, I'd eventually come out in Gena's backyard.

We had kidded around a few times about how sometime I'd sneak out some night, go through the woods, and climb the rose trellis at the back of her house up to her bedroom window. Now here I was about to do just that. But this wasn't kidding around.

Gena had sounded truly terrified. There was something she wanted to tell me. And it sounded to me like someone else didn't want her to say it.

Was she in some kind of real danger? Or was my imagination going wild? I had no choice. I had to find out.

I pushed open the screen door and stepped outside. I was surprised by how cold it was. I could see my breath, gray steam against the black sky.

I headed quickly around the side of the house to the back. The ground was crunchy beneath my sneakers. There had been a heavy dew and I guess it had frozen on the ground. It was a windless night. Everything seemed very still, so still it was almost unreal. It was silent except for my sneakers crunching over the hard, frozen ground.

Our backyard slopes steeply down for a while before it levels off. Once I got down the hill, I started jogging until I reached the woods. I knew if I just kept going straight for a while, I'd see some lights from houses on the other side of the woods, and then I could make my way to Gena's backyard.

The trick, of course, was to keep going perfectly straight. It wasn't easy in these woods. There was no path, of course, and sometimes thick clumps of trees or high weeds would block your way and force you to veer one way or the other.

It seemed to grow colder as I stepped into the woods. I had to slow down. The dead leaves that blanketed the ground were up over my ankles, wet and slick. I kept stumbling over small rocks and upraised roots hidden by the leaves.

The flashlight flickered and grew dimmer. I shook it, but it didn't help. The light had gone from white to yellow, and it was so dim, I could barely see two feet in front of me.

Something scampered past my feet. My heart skipped a beat. I saw the leaves move as if they were jumping out of the way.

"Whoa," I said aloud.

So, big deal. So there were animals running around in the woods. Big surprise. I forced my heart to stop pounding like that, pushed some tall reeds out of my way, and kept walking.

I suddenly remembered a story about the Fear Street woods a guy named Arnie Tobin had told me at school. It was about these five teenagers who went camping out in the woods, sort of on a dare. Everyone bet them they could never spend the whole night in the Fear Street woods, and they bet they could.

So that night they set up two tents and built a campfire and were about to cook supper. The next thing anyone knew, these five teenagers came running out of the woods, knocking on doors of houses, terrified out of their skulls.

They said some kind of monster had attacked the camp. None of them could really describe it. They said it looked sort of like a guinea pig or white rat— only a hundred times bigger! They said it was bigger than a full-grown horse!

They were five terrified kids, Tobin told me, but most people didn't believe them. The cops came to take them home. And *they* didn't believe them, either.

The next day, the five teenagers went back to the campsite with their parents to retrieve all their stuff. And *finally* someone believed them! Because when they got to the camp, everyone could see that one of the canvas tents had been gnawed to bits. All of the food had been eaten—even the unopened cans of beans. It seems the creature—whatever it was—had chewed right through the cans!

Whoa!

I wished I hadn't suddenly remembered that story. Now, every rustle, every crack of a twig made me spin around, expecting to see a giant rat lumbering toward me, its enormous teeth bared, ready to chew me to pieces like a tin can.

I stopped and listened. Silence.

I raised the flashlight, shook it, trying to get more light from it, and shone it through a clump of low shrubs ahead of me. Nothing moved.

The silence was too eerie. I wished a dog would bark or an owl would hoot—anything. I suddenly felt as if I were walking on the moon or on a distant, uninhabited planet.

And then I realized that I had completely lost my sense of direction.

Which way was Gena's house? Was I still heading in the right direction? Which way was my house?

I turned off the flashlight. It was no use to me now, and I decided I'd better save the batteries. I waited for my eyes to adjust to the darkness. Then I slowly turned, peering into the distance, looking for a light, any light.

There was only darkness.

I'm lost, I thought.

But just as I thought that and a cold shudder ran down my back, the trees seemed to light up. I looked up to see that the moon had emerged from a bank of rolling clouds. I stared at it gratefully. I had been walking with the moon on my right when I entered the woods. Now if I kept it on my right, I would be going in the same direction.

I began to feel good again. Well, not good. Let's say that I got some of my confidence back. I tried the flashlight. It had completely died. I moved forward, guided only by the moon.

I was moving pretty quickly, jogging over the blanket of wet leaves. It's amazing how well you can see at night in the woods. I never realized that human eyes were so good in the dark.

That's what I was thinking about when I heard the footsteps behind me.

I knew at once that they were footsteps. And I knew at once that they weren't mine. It was so still, so airless, so silent in the woods, that I could hear every sound.

I stopped and listened, suddenly feeling very afraid. The footsteps were moving quickly, growing closer. My legs suddenly felt weak and wobbly. I tried to figure out if it was a four-legged creature or a two-legged creature running toward me. But it was impossible to tell.

I saw the giant white rat again in my mind. What kind of footsteps would that creature make as it scurried after its prey?

Prey?

Somehow I shook off my fear and started running. I made sure to keep the moon on my right so I wouldn't get completely turned around.

Even though I was running as fast as I could now, keeping my arms in front of my face to shield myself from low tree limbs, the footsteps grew closer. Whoever—or whatever—was pursuing me was closing the gap.

I thought of turning and stopping, facing whoever it was. But I quickly decided that was stupid.

I started to run again—and cried out as my feet went out from under me. Suddenly I was sliding down, down, off balance, out of control. *"Help!"* I cried as I fell.

I realized at once that I had fallen into some kind of a trap.

chapter
14

*R*oger seemed to be walking toward town. He took long strides and never looked back. I had to hurry to keep him in sight. It was a very dark night. The streetlights on Fear Street were out, as usual, and the moon had disappeared behind a heavy cloud bank.

Wisps of fog felt wet and cold against my face as I moved silently, staying against the hedges and shrubs that lined the street. I wished he would slow down just a little. But the fact that he was in such a hurry made me even more suspicious.

He turned left on Mill Road and picked up his pace. A car went by, its headlights glaring into my eyes nearly blinding me for a few seconds. I ducked behind a low evergreen and waited for the yellow spots to disappear.

When I walked back onto the road, he had gotten even farther ahead. I started to jog. I didn't want to lose him in the darkness. The ground was hard and wet. My sneakers moved silently. The only sounds were the rush of wind from the north and the occasional low rumble of a passing car.

Roger turned onto Hawthorne Drive and looked from side to side. I dived for the ground and crawled behind a mailbox, hoping that he hadn't spotted me. When I looked up, I saw nothing but dark trees. He was gone.

I climbed to my feet quickly and crept forward. There was a small coffee shop called Alma's on Hawthorne, where a lot of local college kids sat around studying and drinking coffee till all hours. I wondered if he was headed there.

As I drew closer, his tall, loping form came into view again. Yes, he was heading into Alma's. But why? He definitely didn't plan to study. He wasn't carrying any books.

He was probably just meeting a friend. And I was out here on this cold, wet night, walking around in the dark, wasting my time.

Well, Mark would have a good laugh at my expense. I pictured Mark, sitting at home, waiting for Captain Farraday to call. My poor brother. He was already in an emotional state because of Mom and Dad. Gena's breaking up with him had really sent him over the edge.

I probably should've stayed home with him. But it was too late now.

After Roger entered Alma's, I waited a few minutes. Then I walked up to the window and peered inside. It wasn't very crowded. Only a few booths were filled, the usual college students and a few solitary old people nursing steaming white mugs of coffee.

I couldn't see Roger. I figured he must be sitting

way in the back or in one of the side booths by the counter. Should I go in?

I'd come this far. I decided what the heck, I might as well just take a peek and see what Roger was up to.

I pulled my jacket hood up to hide my face and stepped into the coffee shop. It was very warm inside and smelled of bacon and frying grease. I kept my head down inside the hood and walked slowly toward the row of booths. Ducking down behind the wall of the first booth, I poked my head around the side and looked for Roger.

He was sitting in the last booth in the back of the restaurant. He was busily talking and gesturing with his hands. I had to take a few steps closer to see whom he was talking to.

It was the man with the white-blond hair, the man from the van. They were both talking very excitedly. Both of them looked upset. The man from the van kept slapping his hand on the table as he talked.

So Roger *was* lying, I thought. This little trip of mine hadn't been a waste of time, after all. He had lied about the van, and he must have been lying about the gun. Roger and this white-haired guy were working together to—to do what?

Whatever it was, I knew it had something to do with Mom and Dad.

I leaned against the back of the booth and watched as Roger took a piece of paper out of his pocket and started drawing something on it. He was drawing and pointing to parts of the drawing. What was it? A map?

I would've done anything to see what it was. But I knew I couldn't go any closer without being seen. I turned to see a fat waitress glaring at me from behind the counter. I guess I must have looked pretty suspicious.

I decided to get out of there. I had seen enough to prove that Roger was a liar and that we had to tell Captain Farraday about him as quickly as possible.

Holding my hood up, I turned and started to leave when a hand grabbed my shoulder. A voice called, "Hey, Cara!"

"Ouch!" I cried out more in surprise than pain. But the hand dug into my shoulder as if trying to pin me there in place.

I spun around to see who it was. It was Roger.

"Spying on me again?" he asked, not loosening his grip on my shoulder. His eyes burned into mine.

He's dangerous, I thought.

I never realized it. I never even seriously considered it. But he's dangerous.

"Ouch. You're hurting me, Roger," I said. My hood fell back on my shoulders. Great disguise!

He let go of my shoulder, but his expression didn't change. "Sorry. I didn't mean to."

Yes, he did. Of course he meant to.

I looked past him to his companion back in the booth, who was studying me, a tight-lipped frown on his pale, white face.

To my surprise, Roger suddenly smiled, as if he had regained control of his anger. He saw me staring at his friend. He took my elbow and led me back to the booth. "Oh . . . uh . . . Cara, this is Dr. Murdoch," Roger said, sliding back into the booth. "He's my . . . faculty advisor."

Yeah, right. Sure, Roger. And I'm the Queen of England.

"Nice to meet you," I said, not even pretending to mean it.

"Dr." Murdoch gave me a wide, phony grin.

"We were just meeting about my major," Roger added. What a rotten liar! He saw me looking at the piece of paper he'd been writing on, and folded it in half. His eyes turned cold again. "So what are you doing here?"

"I'm . . . meeting a friend here." My story wasn't any worse than his. "But it looks like she's not coming," I quickly added. "See you later."

"Nice to meet you," the so-called Dr. Murdoch called after me as I ran down the aisle and out of the restaurant.

I didn't breathe until I was out the door and outside. I bumped into two guys coming in, and they both laughed as I continued to run down the street.

It felt even colder out. A fine, misty rain was falling. I pulled my hood up, this time for warmth. My heart was pounding. I felt like such an idiot.

Oh, well. The first thing I was going to do, I decided, when I got home was to run up to Roger's room, take that pistol out of his desk, and hide it somewhere.

Roger frightened me. The idea that he had a loaded pistol right in my house was even more frightening. Anyway, I had proven that Roger was a liar. And so was his friend Murdoch. . . . He told Mark and me he didn't even know Roger!

I suddenly felt very afraid. I started to jog toward home. But I wouldn't be safe there either, I realized.

My parents were gone. And Mark and I shared the house with a liar who had a gun.

Feeling chilled through and through, I started to jog faster. If only Mark and I knew somebody in town, had some relatives, had some place to go . . .

I was about two blocks from home when I realized there was a car following me.

chapter
15

Okay, okay, Mark. Cool it, man.

Take a deep breath and cool it.

It was a very crude trap. Just a deep pit covered over with leaves. The hole wasn't more than six feet deep and ten or twelve feet wide.

You can handle it. You don't have to panic. You're not trapped here forever. You can pull yourself out. Just reach up with your arms and hoist yourself up. You can do it.

Go ahead. Take another deep breath. Then get back up on your feet and get moving again.

That's how I talked myself calm. That's how I got my heart to stop pounding like the drums on a Def Leppard record and got myself standing up.

But as soon as I pulled myself out of the pit and stood up, still unsteady, still a little panicked, I wished I hadn't. Because the creature that had been following me came charging at me.

It was so dark I couldn't see what it was.

I just heard it running toward me, felt its powerful forelegs hit my chest, heard a low growl, and inhaled its hot, sour breath as I fell back into the pit.

"Help!"

I don't know why I screamed. There was no one around.

I was flat on my back. With another low growl, the creature jumped down on top of me. It wrapped its jaws around my left wrist and started to clamp down.

Despite my terror, I began to think more clearly. I realized I was wrestling with a large dog, some sort of shepherd.

"Down, boy! *Down!* Go home!"

I didn't recognize my voice. It was the voice of a terrified child.

It was certainly high enough for dogs to hear. But this dog chose not to listen. I pulled my wrist from his grasp, spun away, and crawled away from the animal to the corner of the pit.

The creature circled toward me now, keeping its head down, its growl a low, menacing rumble.

It's the biggest dog I've ever seen, I thought, backing away as it circled. What is it doing out here? Is it a wild dog?

And am I its dinner?

No. It wasn't wild. I could see that it was wearing a collar. Something was hanging from the collar under the dog's chin.

"Down, boy. Good dog. Good dog."

It lowered its head and pulled back its lips to reveal a mouthful of teeth. The teeth, long and pointed, seemed to gleam in the moonlight. And I knew I'd never forget them.

"Good dog. Good dog. Go home, boy."

I was muttering those words over and over like an idiot. This dog couldn't go home. This dog *was* home. The Fear Street woods were his home. And he was about to show me how good he was at protecting his home.

Never let a dog see that you're afraid of him. For some reason those words from my dad flashed through my mind. That may have been the dumbest thing my dad ever said to me!

How do you let the dog know you're not afraid of him when you're frozen on your knees in a pit, trembling all over, squeaking in a high-pitched voice for him to go home like a nice doggy?

I didn't have time to think about that for long. The dog uttered a loud groan and leapt at my face. I ducked. I could feel his weight as he slid over my back, yipping in surprise.

He landed hard, but was back on his feet immediately.

Again he lunged for me. I fell backward, out of his way.

I tried scrambling up the side of the hole, but fell back, landing on the dog's back. He roared out his unhappiness and tried to struggle out from under me, but I grabbed his head under the chin and started to pull up.

His fur was hot and wet. I inhaled the most powerful dog smell I'd ever smelled. It clogged my nose.

I held my breath. I thought I was going to be sick.

The dog started twisting and turning, trying to get out of my grip. But I held on with both hands, hugging the dog tighter and tighter, squeezing its middle as I pulled its head back.

Its growl turned into a howl of pain, but I didn't let go. I was losing my hold. My hands were slipping off the wet fur. I exhaled and took a deep breath, inhaling the heavy, repulsive odor.

The dog gave a hard tug. I stumbled forward, digging my knee into its back, pulling up its head, pulling, pulling with all the strength I had left.

Suddenly I heard a loud crack.

Startled, I let go and fell backward against the dirt wall of the pit.

I had broken its neck.

The dog stopped howling.

It stared at me in silence, a look of surprise, a look of pain. Then its eyes closed, and it slumped to the ground with a thud.

I stared down at it, gasping for breath. I wiped my forehead with my hand. I was covered in sweat—cold, cold sweat. I could smell the disgusting dog smell on my hand.

Then for a long time I just stood there, leaning against the side of the hole, staring at the dead dog. I kept hearing that horrifying crack again and again. And I saw the surprised look on the dog's face, that look of pain, of total defeat.

I bent down to make sure the dog was dead. Holding my breath, I rolled the big creature onto its back—and saw the object that was attached to the front of its collar.

It was a white monkey head.

I gasped in surprise.

This didn't make any sense. I grabbed the monkey

head and held it in my hand to make sure I wasn't seeing things! What was the same object I had found in my parents' bedroom doing around the neck of a dog in the middle of the Fear Street woods?

Then something else caught my eye. Part of a chain leash was still attached to the collar. I followed the chain to the end and discovered a broken link. The dog had obviously broken its leash.

As I climbed out of the pit, I saw a wooden stake just a few yards away. I walked over to it and, sure enough, the other part of the chain leash was attached to the stake.

So the dog had originally been placed near the trap. It must have broken away a little while before I came on the scene. It saw me approaching its spot and chased after me.

Chased after me without barking.

It had obviously been trained to sneak up on people, to attack quietly.

Someone wanted to keep people away from this part of the woods.

But why?

All of my muscles ached. I shivered. I'll never feel normal again, I thought.

Looking around, trying to clear my head, I suddenly realized I was on the edge of a large, round clearing. The moon was right overhead now, shining brightly, so brightly I could see dozens of shoe prints in the soft dirt.

It looked as if a lot of people had been here recently.

Obviously the trap and the attack dog were here to keep people out of this clearing. But why?

"I've got to get away from here," I said aloud, feeling chilled and frightened.

I knew there were houses at the edge of the woods. But, standing here I felt far away from civilization. Take a few steps into these woods and anything can happen, I thought. This is a different world, a world without any rules.

I had to do something to stop these grim thoughts.

Gena. Remember Gena. I reminded myself to think about Gena, about how upset she had sounded on the phone.

I suddenly remembered what I was doing out here. I had to get to Gena's. I had to talk with her, find out why our phone conversation had been cut off. I had to make things right with her again.

I thought about Cara, out somewhere following Roger. What a crazy idea! I wondered if she was home yet. I wondered if Mom and Dad had come home, or if the policeman had any news for us.

"I'll call her from Gena's," I said aloud.

I walked a bit, my legs unsteady at first. Eventually I began to feel stronger. I saw a light through the trees, a pale gray-green light, shimmering like a firefly between two trees.

A house. I began running toward the light, ignoring the thorns and tall, spiny weeds and upraised tree roots that tried to slow me down.

A few moments later, I was standing at the edge of Gena's backyard. It wasn't far from the mysterious clearing, I realized. Trying to catch my breath, I stared up at the dim light behind the shade of her bedroom window.

Was she up there? I couldn't tell. The lights were on

in the den downstairs, and I could see the flickering glow from the TV screen. Someone walked past the window. It was Gena's dad. I moved closer, being careful to stay in the dark shadows by the side of the big garage.

Her dad was standing in front of the TV, sipping from a can. I watched him walk back to the couch and sit down. Then I looked up at Gena's room again.

Could I really do this? My eyes followed the tall, wooden rose trellis down from just under Gena's second-story window to the ground. Of course the roses were all gone, but the long, thorny vines remained.

I walked quickly over to the trellis and took hold of it. It seemed sturdy enough. It would probably hold my weight.

I grabbed its sides with my hands, careful to avoid the thick, thorny vines, and put a foot on the bottom slat. I leaned over and peered into the den window just to make sure Gena's father was still on the couch in the den. He was.

So I started to climb. One step at a time. The trellis shook a little, but it was sturdier than it looked.

I was about a third of the way up when my hand slipped, and I started to fall.

chapter

16

As I continued to jog home, I heard the car approach. The headlights lit up the street in front of me. I slowed down and waited for the car to pass me.

But it didn't pass.

Mark was right. I never should have gone out of the house tonight. I started running faster and the car started moving faster, too.

What was going on? I turned around but couldn't see beyond the bright yellow headlights.

I didn't know what to do. Why wasn't the car passing me? If it was someone I knew, why didn't they catch up to me? Or honk or something?

I decided to turn and run back the other way, past the car. In the time it would take the car to turn around, I figured, I could get away.

So I spun around and, shielding my eyes from the headlights, started to run at full speed. The car squealed to a stop.

"Cara! Hey, stop! Cara!"

It was a familiar voice.

I stopped. A man climbed out from the driver's side.

I recognized the big blue Caprice. Then I recognized Captain Farraday.

"Captain Farraday! Hi!" I cried, so relieved.

"I wasn't sure if it was you or not," he said, walking up to me quickly, his boots clicking on the pavement. "Hope I didn't frighten you. I was on my way to your house."

"Do you have any news about my parents?"

The streetlight was reflected in his deep, blue eyes. He looked very tired. He shook his head. "No. Not yet. I was wondering if you heard anything."

"No," I said, sighing.

"Hey, don't look like that," he said, putting a gloved hand on the shoulder of my jacket. "We don't have any *bad* news, right?"

"Right," I muttered. "But we don't have any good news, either."

He led me toward the car. "You have to keep thinking good thoughts," he said. "My men are on the case. Your parents will turn up soon."

I didn't say anything. I couldn't hide my disappointment.

"I need to get a photo of them from you," he said. "I'll put out an APB, get a copy of it to every police department in the state. Can you think of anything else, any kind of clue or information that might be at all helpful to me?" He was so tall, he leaned his head down when he talked to me.

"Well . . . let me think . . ." I said.

"Why don't I give you a lift home and you can think

about it on the way? And you can give me that photo. My men are all on the case. I also alerted the newspaper. Sometimes people phone in tips to them.''

He held the front door open and I slid in. I'd never been in a police car before. I was a little disappointed to see that the Caprice wasn't a police car at all. It was just a regular car. The radio suddenly came to life and spit out a burst of static and then a brief message. It was a police radio, the only evidence that this was a police car.

As he drove me home, I told Farraday about Roger, about Roger's pistol, and Murdoch and the gray van. I expected him to say something, but he kept his eyes straight ahead on the road and didn't react at all.

"Do you think Roger might know something about my parents?" I asked finally.

"Maybe. I'll have to check out this Roger and—what did you say the other guy's name was?"

"Roger called him Dr. Murdoch."

"I'll check him out, too. Anything else, Cara? Anything else at all that might be helpful to us?"

We pulled up the drive. The house was dark. I was annoyed that Mark hadn't turned the porch light on for me.

"I can't think of anything. Nothing at all," I told Farraday. I opened the door and started to get out. "Oh, yeah. Wait. There *is* one other thing."

He turned to look at me. "Yes?"

"Mark and I found this strange thing in my parents' bedroom. It was a little monkey head; a little white monkey head with rhinestone eyes. Do you think that could be a clue?"

Again he didn't react. "Maybe," he said quietly.

"It doesn't ring any bell with me, but maybe it means something. I'll ask around at the station. Do you have it? It might be a good idea to get it to the lab. They can do a check on it."

I ran into the house. I didn't see Mark. I hurried upstairs and pulled a fairly recent photo of my parents out of the album they keep in their bed table. Then I searched around for the white monkey head. I couldn't find it. I'd have to ask Mark what he did with it.

Back outside, I handed Farraday the photograph. "Thanks for the lift," I said glumly. "And for all your help."

"Get some sleep," he said. "I know it's hard, but it'll help."

"I'll try," I said.

"You'll hear from me as soon as I know anything at all. And, Cara—you've got my number. Call me anytime, day or night. Call me for any reason, hear?"

"Thanks," I said. "That makes me feel a lot better."

"I'm glad," he said, and a smile almost broke out beneath his bushy mustache.

I hurried into the house, closed the door behind me, locked it, and called, "Mark! Mark, where are you?"

No answer.

"Mark, are you upstairs?" I shouted.

Still no answer.

I searched the living room and den and then went upstairs to see if he had gone to bed. He wasn't home.

Returning to the living room, I was overcome with a feeling of dread. First Mom and Dad disappeared. Now Mark. Was he gone, too?

Maybe he left a note. I ran into the kitchen and

checked the refrigerator. No. I checked the pad by the telephone. No note.

Now Mark is missing, I thought.

No. He probably went over to Gena's. That's right. Of course he did.

I picked up the phone receiver. I was going to call Gena's house to talk to him. But then I thought better of it. Mark wouldn't want his little sister calling at Gena's to check up on him. Besides, I had no news for him about Mom and Dad, no news at all.

I decided to go into the den and watch TV until Mark got home. Maybe it would take my mind off everything.

I was crossing the living room when I saw the lights climbing up the wall—twin spotlights moving slowly. It took me a while to realize they were car headlights.

Someone had pulled into the driveway.

Was it Mark? Was it Mom and Dad?

chapter
17

I knew I was going down. I grabbed frantically at the trellis but my hand caught a thorny vine. As I dropped, the big thorns cut through my left palm.

I didn't have time to cry out. I landed hard on my back. It knocked the wind out of me. I thought I was dead. There's no worse feeling in the world. You can't breathe. You know you're never going to breathe again. I must've passed out or something. I'm not sure. Everything became bright red and then yellow, blindingly bright yellow.

I don't know how long I was lying there on the ground, probably not as long as it seemed to me. The bright colors faded away. Then I realized I was breathing again.

My left hand throbbed with pain. I held it up close to my face to examine it. The thorns had cut two deep lines down the center of my palm. My hand was bleeding pretty badly, the blood seeping out in two straight lines.

I looked up to the top of the trellis. The light was still on in Gena's room. I decided I had to try the climb again. Once inside, Gena could find something I could wrap my hand in to stop the bleeding.

Gena was so close. I wanted to see her. I *had* to see her. I thought about her long, black hair, about her smile, about the way she felt sitting on my lap on the couch with her warm arms around me, and I pulled myself up the trellis, slowly at first, then more quickly as I gained confidence.

Gena's bedroom window was a foot above the trellis. It was closed. I couldn't tell whether it was locked or not. I tapped on the glass and waited for her to come to the window.

The trellis creaked under my weight. Suddenly I wasn't so sure it could hold me.

Where was Gena?

I tapped again on the window, this time a little louder. No response.

I leaned forward, reached up, and pushed the window with all my strength. It didn't budge.

I was trapped. I couldn't get into the house. And any second, the trellis was going to fall and take me down with it.

Taking a deep breath, I reached up and pushed with both hands against the window frame. This time the window slid up a few inches. What a relief! It wasn't locked.

A few seconds later, I scrambled headfirst into Gena's bedroom. It wasn't exactly a romantic entrance, but at least I'd made it—and the trellis was still standing.

"Gena?" I whispered.

I looked around the room, which was lit by a single lamp on Gena's dresser. She wasn't there. In fact, it looked as if she hadn't been there at all.

The bed was made. Her stuffed-animal collection was lined up along the wall over the bed. Her backpack was hung over the back of her desk chair. Her desk was totally neat, some papers and pencils stacked up in a corner. The carpet looked as if it had just been vacuumed that day. You know the way rugs stand up after they've been vacuumed. The only footprints I could see in the rug were mine.

I crept over to the closet door, which had hundreds of photos taped to it from top to bottom. There were snapshots of Gena and her dad; of her mother, who lived outside Detroit; snapshots of people I didn't recognize; and lots of photos of her favorite movie stars cut out of magazines. I was pleased to see that the photo I had given her, my class photo from last year, was taped up right above the doorknob, right between Dennis Quaid and Tom Cruise.

Suddenly feeling tired, I sat down on the edge of her bed, careful not to rest my bleeding hand on the white bedspread. Where was she? If she wasn't here, why was the light on?

It's pretty late. She'll probably be up soon, I told myself. I decided I'd just wait for her.

But I quickly decided that was stupid. I couldn't just sit there. For one thing, I had to so something to stop my hand from bleeding.

I got up and walked over to her dresser. I pulled open the top drawer. It was filled with underwear and socks and stuff. I pulled out a long, white wool knee sock and wrapped it around and around my hand. Gena won't mind, I thought.

But where was she?

When she'd called she sounded so upset, so completely freaked. She couldn't be sitting downstairs watching TV with her dad now.

Holding the sock tightly around my hand, I walked back over to the closet door and pulled it open. It was the neatest closet I'd ever seen. All of her clothes were hung up. Her sweaters were folded neatly on the top shelf. I had no idea she was such a neat freak.

I closed the closet and was heading back toward the bed when something caught my eye. There was something shiny down on the rug at the foot of the bed.

I kicked it out from under the bed with the toe of my sneaker, then bent down to pick it up. I carried it over to the lamp on the dresser and examined it.

I couldn't believe it. It was a carved white monkey head.

It was identical to the others. The rhinestone eyes sparkled and seemed to peer out at me. The monkey's mouth was pulled back in an eerie grin.

What was this thing? And why was it popping up everywhere I went?

Suddenly I had a chilling thought. Was this the *same* monkey head?

Had it somehow followed me?

I remembered waking up and finding the monkey head beside my bed when I had no memory of carrying it to my room. Was I holding the same monkey head now, staring into the same blank, glowing eyes?

Don't be a dork, Mark. You've been watching too many old "Twilight Zones."

I didn't have any more time to think about it. I heard footsteps in the hall. They were approaching quickly.

I tucked the monkey head into my jeans pocket and looked around for a place to hide. But there wasn't any.

The footsteps were right outside the bedroom door.

"Gena?" I whispered happily.

And her father stepped into the room.

My eyes dropped from his startled face to the small, silver pistol in his hand.

I didn't hear any more tonight until an hour's sleep
hours through the hall. Then there was creaking cupboard,
a noise of the cooking heated into my years. I quaked and
jerked and stood very still to tone. But there he was in
any

chapter

18

"*M*ark!" he cried. He tossed the pistol onto the bed. "I could've shot you! I—I thought you were a burglar!"

"Sorry." The word choked in my throat.

Dr. Rawlings was a big man—so big he blocked the entire doorway. He was dressed in a gray-and-white running suit. It must have been the biggest size they made! He had black hair like Gena's, only it had thinned back, giving him a high forehead above his bushy black eyebrows.

He was very muscular, too. Big biceps. He looked as if he worked out. I'd never noticed that till now, as I stared back at him, watching the look on his face change from anger to confusion.

I'm in trouble now, I thought. But how much trouble?

He took a couple of steps toward me. For an instant, I thought he was going to fight me. It's crazy the things you think when you're in total panic.

Then I realized he was staring at the white sock wrapped around my hand. Blood had soaked through in several places. It looked really gross. I lowered my hand to my side.

"Mark . . . I feel so bad," he said. "The gun. Good heavens! You should have told me you were here."

"Dr. Rawlings, I—" I just stopped. I didn't know what to say. I mean, what can you say? "I'm sorry. I didn't mean to frighten you. I wanted to talk to Gena, and—"

"What happened to your hand?" he asked. He had a very deep voice. It was usually booming. He talked very loudly and shouted a lot, not from anger but from enthusiasm. But now he was talking so softly, I could barely hear him. He was really freaked that he'd almost shot me.

I reluctantly held up my injured hand. "I cut it," I said. "Listen, I want to explain. I—"

"You came to see Gena?" Dr. Rawlings sat down heavily on her bed. The mattress was soft and sagged nearly to the floor under his weight. He picked up the pistol, then put it down again.

"Well, yeah. She called and—"

He shifted his weight on the bed. "Gena's very upset, Mark," he said, looking up at the ceiling. "I told you that when you were here earlier."

"I know. I'm upset, too," I said. That was the truth, for sure.

"Ah, young love," Dr. Rawlings sighed, and shook his head. He stood up quickly. He moved like a much lighter man. "Sorry, Mark. I don't mean to be facetious. I know this is serious for you and Gena. But even so, you shouldn't have sneaked in."

"I know. I'm really sorry. Uh . . . where is Gena, anyway?" I asked, pulling the sock tighter around my aching hand.

"She went to her cousin's. She was so upset, she thought it might be a good idea to go away."

"Her cousin's? The one upstate?"

He nodded.

"She went without her book bag?" It just happened to catch my eye. I was so confused at this point, I don't think I really knew *what* I was saying.

Dr. Rawlings chuckled. "I *told* you she was very upset. I don't think her book bag was the first thing on her mind." He walked over and put a big, beefy hand on my shoulder. "Want me to take a look at that hand? I *am* a doctor, after all."

I pulled the hand away. "No. No, thanks. It's not really serious. I'll bandage it up when I get home." I suddenly just wanted to get out of there, to get home and think this all through.

I looked to the window. It was still wide open. Mr. Rawlings was looking at it, too. Now he knew how I got inside. If he didn't know already.

I felt really embarrassed. I had broken into his house and he was being so nice about it.

"Come on downstairs and go out the door this time," he said, guiding me to the bedroom door with his hand on my shoulder.

"I'm really sorry," I said. "I shouldn't have—"

He squeezed my shoulder, probably a little harder than he realized. "Don't apologize. It's okay. I understand these things. I'm sorry, too. I'm sorry about you and Gena. She's very unpredictable sometimes. I hope I didn't frighten you with that gun."

"You're not going to tell my parents or anything?"

My parents. I had forgotten about them. And about Cara. What time was it? She had probably gotten back a while ago—and I hadn't left her a note!

"No. Not this time," he said, leading the way down the stairs. Then he added, "I'm looking forward to meeting your parents sometime."

I apologized again to Dr. Rawlings and stepped out into the cold. "Take care, Mark," he said softly. He reached out, took my hand, and shook it.

"Thank you," I said. I didn't know what else to say. I felt really awkward.

I turned and walked quickly down the drive. My hand throbbed. The white sock was soaked with blood. This time, I decided, I would definitely take the *front* way home!

chapter

19

Who had pulled up the drive? I tore across the living room, took a deep breath, and pulled open the front door. "Oh."

"Thanks a lot, Cara. Some greeting," Lisa Blume said.

"Sorry," I said quickly, still unable to hide my disappointment.

"Who were you expecting? Tom Cruise?" Lisa asked, giving me her customary half sneer as she stepped into the front hallway.

"No. It's just that—well . . . come in," I said. "I'm really glad to see you."

"Yeah. I can tell," she said sarcastically. "Listen, I thought maybe we could go over our history notes together. But if this is a bad time . . ."

"It's a bad time," I said, deciding to tell Lisa what was going on. "But I'm glad you're here, anyway." I led her into the den. She plopped down on the couch and tossed her backpack on the floor.

We're a strange pair of friends, I thought, watching her lean down to open her backpack and pull out a notebook. We look like two different species. I'm so blond and immature looking, and she has that great, curly black hair and that sly, knowing smile. She looks a lot like Cher, I thought. I really was glad she had stopped by. I needed the company, and she was always funny and sarcastic—just what I needed to take my mind off everything.

"What's with your brother and Gena Rawlings?" Lisa asked, rolling her big, dark eyes. "I couldn't believe them in your living room last night. They didn't even take a *breath!*"

"Well, you're not going to believe *this*, either," I said. "She broke up with him tonight."

Lisa's mouth froze in an O of surprise. "Huh?" she finally managed to say. "Run that by me again, Cara."

"You heard me. She broke up with him."

"But . . . why?"

I shrugged my shoulders. "Mark is in bad shape," I said. "Don't tell him I told you. He went running over there. At least, that's where I think he is."

Lisa pulled at one of her long, black curls. "Weird. Just plain weird."

"Yeah, I know. Mark didn't have a clue."

"Weird," Lisa repeated. She sat there for a while, staring at me thoughtfully. Then she said, "Was Mark chewing gum that night?"

"You mean at the party?"

"Yeah."

"Well, how would I know? What on earth are you talking about, Lisa?"

"Well, I was just thinking about this girl I used to

know. Her name was Shana and she went with a guy named Rick for a short time. And I don't know what made me think of it, but I just remembered that Shana told me about this time she was making out with Rick, and Rick was chewing gum, only Shana didn't know it, and somehow the gum ended up in Shana's mouth.''

"Yuck."

"Yeah. That's what Shana thought. So she broke up with him and never said another word to him.''

"Great story, Lisa," I said, picking up her sarcasm the way anyone did after being around her for a few minutes.

"Well, that's why I was wondering if Mark was chewing gum," Lisa said.

"I've got bigger problems than Mark's love life," I said, sighing.

"Yeah. You've got your *own* love life!" Lisa cracked.

"No, I'm serious," I said.

"So am I."

"My parents are missing," I blurted out.

Lisa didn't react at all. "Go ahead. Next tell me you're growing a second head," she said, staring at me. "I'll believe that, too."

"No. Really, Lisa."

I think she saw by the look on my face that I wasn't kidding. She propped her head up with one hand and stared at me. "They're missing? You mean they didn't come home tonight?"

"Or last night."

"They didn't call?"

I shook my head.

Suddenly all of the humor left Lisa's face. It was as

if a mask had been pulled away and her serious, real face was revealed for the first time. "Did you call the police?"

"Yes. Captain Farraday."

"But he hasn't found them?"

I shook my head. I suddenly felt sick. I had thought that telling Lisa what was happening would make me feel better, but instead, saying it all aloud was making me feel more afraid.

"Do you want to come stay at my place?" Lisa asked. She looked really upset, too.

"No, thanks," I told her. "Mark is—"

"He could come, too. There's plenty of room. Really."

This was so nice of her. I'd only known Lisa for a short while, after all. It wasn't like we were lifelong buddies or anything.

I thanked her again and told her I thought Mark and I would be more comfortable waiting here. Where *was* Mark, anyway? I looked at my watch. It was getting late. I wondered if he'd made up with Gena. If so, he might not be home for quite a while.

I heard a car outside and started to get up. But it drove past without slowing down. Chill out, Cara, I scolded myself. You can't start jumping out of your chair every time a car drives by.

Lisa was looking more upset than me. "They've done this before," I told her, trying to get the grim look off her face.

"Really? They've left for two days without calling?"

"No, not without calling." I stood up. "I'll get my history notes. Let's try to study."

She looked very uncomfortable. "You sure?"

"Yeah. Be good to take my mind off things. Stop me from staring at the clock all night."

She followed me into the living room, where I'd left my backpack. "You know, I think Gary Brandt likes you," she said.

"Huh?"

"Yeah. That's what I heard."

"From who?" I asked. I found my notebook and pulled it out of the bag. Papers fell all over the rug, but I didn't bother to stuff them back in.

"He told a friend of mine that he'd like to go out with you. He's a fox, don't you think?"

"Gary?"

"Yeah. Gary."

"He's okay." For some reason I didn't want to reveal how pleased I was by this news. Gary was a pretty neat guy. "Maybe if my parents don't come back, we'll have another party," I cracked.

Lisa laughed, but it was a halfhearted laugh.

"Not funny, huh?" I squeezed past her and headed back to the den. "Just trying to keep it light."

"If—if my parents just disappeared, I'd *freak!*" Lisa said.

"I'll probably freak after they come back," I told her, plopping down on the leather couch. *If they come back,* I added to myself, and shuddered.

What if I'm an orphan? I thought. What if I'm already an orphan and just don't know it yet?

Who would Mark and I go to live with? Aunt Dorothy? No. She was much too old. Grandma Edna? No. She was too old, too. And she couldn't stand us.

Do teenagers have to go live in an orphanage? I wondered.

"What are you thinking?" Lisa asked.

"Just stupid thoughts," I replied, forcing a smile.

We tried going over our history notes for a while, but I was too distracted to think clearly. I kept looking up at the clock, wondering why Mark wasn't back, and jumping up from the couch every time a car drove past.

Finally, we decided that studying just wasn't in the cards. We talked a little more about kids at school. Then Lisa left, telling me again that Mark and I could come stay at her house, and asking me to call as soon as I heard any news.

I felt pretty good for a while after she'd left. I'd made a real friend.

I looked at the clock. It was past eleven. Where was Mark?

I sat down in the living room. What a drab, disgusting room. I got up and started to pace. I walked into the den and gathered up my history notes. I shoved them into my notebook. I started to the kitchen to get another soda—and stopped halfway across the living room.

Roger's gun.

How could I have forgotten my plan? I was going to go upstairs and take it out of his desk and hide it somewhere. I wanted Roger out of our house. But I knew that might take some doing. In the meantime, I didn't want him to have a loaded pistol.

I ran up the stairs and stopped at the landing under the attic. "Roger—are you up there?"

He's always so quiet, he could've come in while Lisa and I were talking. There was no reply. I called again, and again no reply.

So I climbed the narrow stairs and let myself into his room.

I fumbled around until I found the switch on his desk lamp, and clicked it on. The room was empty. Roger had tossed a shirt and a pair of chinos on the cot. Everything else looked the same.

I bent down quickly and pulled out the bottom desk drawer.

A creak.

Was that a footstep? Was that Roger returning?

I stopped and listened. Another creak. It was just this stupid old house making noises.

Still listening for any sounds outside the tiny room, I lifted out the underwear from the bottom drawer. Then I reached for the small pistol.

My hand couldn't find it, so I leaned over and looked into the drawer.

Then I let out a little gasp as I realized the pistol was gone.

chapter

20

*T*hursday went by in a blur. Mark and I were too tired and too lost in our own thoughts to say hardly anything over breakfast. Somehow we got ourselves to school. My body was there, but my mind was in a million other places.

After school, we drove home together. Mark glumly told me about what had happened to him in the woods, about the trap near the clearing and the dog that had been trained to attack silently.

"I—I killed it, broke its back, I think," Mark said. I could see that he was still badly shaken. Then he told me about Gena's dad, how he had almost shot Mark.

As we drove, I told Mark about Roger and Murdoch at the coffee shop, and about the gun being missing from Roger's drawer.

"We've got to tell Farraday about Roger," Mark said, pulling up the drive. "After last night, Roger knows that we're suspicious of him. That could make him even more dangerous."

"I already told Farraday," I said.

We pulled into the drive. "Call Farraday again," Mark said, sounding a little desperate. "See if he's done anything."

I ran into the house to call Farraday. I saw Mark heading out to the backyard. I knew what he was going to do—shoot arrows into the target until his arm was tired.

I threw down my books and crept to the front stairs. I went halfway up, listening for any sounds that might reveal that Roger was home. Finally, I decided to take a more direct approach. "Roger—are you up there?" I shouted.

No reply. Feeling relieved, I went to the kitchen phone to call Captain Farraday.

I slammed the phone down in disgust when I realized that it was dead again. "Mark, the stupid phone is out again!" I shouted through the kitchen window.

He didn't hear me. Or at least he pretended not to hear me. He fired off another arrow, then another, staring intently, never taking his eyes from the target.

A few minutes later, I went out back. Mark was just firing off the last arrow in the quiver. "Feel better?" I asked.

"No," he replied, frowning.

We drove to the mall and shared a pizza for dinner. Neither of us felt much like talking. Afterward, we glumly stepped out into the cold, blustery night. The air was heavy and wet. It felt as if it might snow.

We were halfway home when I remembered something that changed *everything*.

"Wally," I said.

Mark, driving with one hand, kept his eyes on the road. "Huh? What did you say?"

"Wally!"

He looked annoyed. "That's what I thought you said. Is there more to that sentence?"

"I don't know his last name," I said, my mind desperately searching for it. I was excited. I knew I had just remembered something very important. Now, if I could just calm down enough to think clearly and remember . . .

"Wally who? You mean on 'Leave It to Beaver'?" Mark turned onto Fear Street, and it suddenly became much darker. The streetlights were still out.

"No. I mean Mom and Dad's friend. Wally Wilburn!"

Even in the pitch black I could see Mark's mouth drop open. "From work! That guy who called a lot and invited them to go bowling. You're right, Cara! Wally Wilburn. That's his name."

He roared up the drive and stopped with a loud squeal. "We'll get their phone book. I'll bet they wrote his phone number in their phone book."

We both slammed car doors and went running into the house. "This guy Wally—he can *prove* they worked at Cranford Industries," I said. "And once we've proved that, we can . . ." I stopped. I didn't know *what* the next step would be.

"Let's just talk to Wally," Mark said.

We ran into the kitchen, and Mark grabbed the little phone book. "Let's see. . . ." Mark squinted up his face. His finger moved down the ruled pages of the little phone book. "Here it is. Wally Wilburn."

"Where does he live?"

Mark's face fell. "Just a phone number. No address."

I picked up the phone. Still dead. "No problem," I said. "Let's find the area phone book. His address is bound to be in there."

"Unless he has an unlisted number," Mark said dejectedly.

"Mr. Pessimist. You sure give up easily," I said, pulling the big phone directory off the shelf and turning to the back. It only took me a few seconds to find the listing for W. Wilburn. "He lives at Two Thirty-one Plum Ridge."

"Where's that? Never heard of it."

I had to laugh. "Mark, you'd make a lousy detective."

"I never said I wanted to be a detective," he grumbled.

I found the area map in the front of the book. Plum Ridge Road was in the next town, about halfway between our house and Cranford Industries. "Come on. Let's go." I pulled him to the back door. "I know how to find it."

"Wally Wilburn," he muttered, shaking his head. "Maybe Wally will help clear up this whole mystery."

It was about a twenty-minute drive to Waynesbridge, the next town. When we reached the outskirts, endless, depressing housing developments of identical, boxlike houses stretching over low hills, I turned off the car radio and began to read street signs.

"What are we going to say to this guy?" Mark asked, suddenly sounding worried.

"Well, I don't think we should come right out and tell him our parents have been missing for three days,"

I said. "We should let him tell us what he knows first. If we come on too strong, we might scare him or something."

"Yeah. That's smart," Mark agreed.

"Let me do the talking," I said.

He nodded.

"Plum Ridge," I said, reading the sign. "That was easy. Turn right."

"Can you read the numbers?" Mark asked, slowing down nearly to a stop.

"Yeah. They're above the front doors. Keep going. It should be in the next block."

Sure enough, the Wilburn house was on the next corner. There was a Ford Mustang in the drive, so we parked on the street and walked up the narrow concrete walk. The air smelled of fresh dirt and fertilizer.

I could hear voices and music from a TV as we stepped onto the front stoop. I knocked loudly, then found the doorbell and rang it. The TV voices stopped abruptly and I heard footsteps, and then the front door was pulled open by a chubby, middle-aged man.

"What are you selling?" he asked. He had a pleasant voice and a very friendly smile beneath a bushy black mustache. He was nearly bald, I saw, except for a thick fringe of black hair around his ears.

"Mr. Wilburn?" I asked, suddenly wondering just what I was going to say.

"You've come to the right place. That just happens to be me. But most folks call me Wally. And who might you be? I haven't seen you around the neighborhood."

"No. We live in Shadyside," Mark said, sounding nervous.

I thought we'd agreed that I would do the talking. I hoped Mark wasn't going to blow it now.

"Well, you've come pretty far to sell raffle tickets." Wally chuckled. He seemed to find himself very amusing.

"No. We're not selling anything. I'm Cara Burroughs, and this is my brother, Mark."

"Burroughs?" He recognized the name immediately. He pushed open the storm door. "Are you Greg and Lucy's kids?"

Mark and I both nodded.

"Well, how are your parents? Where are they? I haven't seen them at work this week."

"You haven't?" Mark blurted out.

"No. They needed me in the C division, so I've been down in the subbasement all week. Haven't picked my head up once. Do your parents miss me?"

Mark and I didn't know how to answer. So I plunged ahead and changed the subject. "We were visiting a friend near here," I said, trying to make it sound believable, "and we stopped here to use your phone, if we could. We forgot to call Mom and Dad. I think they're still at work."

"At this hour?" Wally looked at his watch. "Fanatics." He chuckled. "Good people. But fanatics."

A very thin woman with wavy blond hair walked into the room, surprised to see visitors. She wore faded jeans and a black-and-red Grateful Dead T-shirt. "Hi, hon. These are Greg and Lucy's kids," Wally said. "This is my better half, Margie."

"Nice to meet you," Mark and I said in unison. We both looked at each other uneasily.

"Well, hi," Margie said, giving us a warm smile. "Did you bring your parents?"

"No. They just stopped by to call them," Wally told her.

"Do you have their direct line?" I asked him. "Mark and I haven't memorized it yet."

"No problem." Wally bounced over to a side table and pawed quickly through a stack of magazines and papers. "I work at home sometimes, so I brought a company directory home. Here you go."

He pulled out a stapled directory with a bright yellow cover. I looked quickly at the front. It read: CRANFORD INDUSTRIES PHONE DIRECTORY.

I hoped the Wilburns didn't notice how my hands were trembling as I found the Bs and then searched for my parents' names. There they were, followed by their phone extension.

So. The guy at Cranford, Mr. Marcus, had lied to us. Our parents *did* work at Cranford, just as they had told us. The proof was in our hands. Now we could go to Captain Farraday and tell him to get the truth out of the Marcus character.

I held the book up and showed the listing to Mark, who was standing beside me with his mouth hanging open. I debated whether or not to ask Wally to let us borrow the directory. But I decided that might arouse his suspicions. Besides, we had seen it. And the book was always here if Farraday needed to see it, too.

"Well, thank you very much," I said, handing the directory back and then heading to the door.

"Yeah, thanks," Mark repeated. We were both eager to get out of there.

"Uh . . . aren't you forgetting something?" Wally

asked, looking very amused. We both looked at him blankly. "The phone call. You were going to make a phone call."

"Oh. Right!" How embarassing.

We went through the motions. I dialed my parents' direct line and let it ring several times. "No answer. They must be on their way home," I told Wally.

It took us a few more minutes of thank-yous and nice-to-meet-yous to get out the door. "He must think we're pretty weird," Mark said, sliding behind the steering wheel.

"I don't care," I said. "We just proved that our parents didn't lie to us. They did work at Cranford."

"Did that receptionist at Cranford lie to us?"

"No," I said. "Mom and Dad's names definitely weren't on her computer screen. It only takes a second to delete a name from a computer file. But that big shot Marcus *did* lie."

"Why would he do that?" Mark asked, pulling away from the curb.

"I don't know. But the police will help us find out," I said, feeling very excited about our detective work. "Let's go find Captain Farraday. We've got a lot to tell him!"

The twenty-minute drive back to Shadyside seemed to take forever. Back on the Mill Road, Mark suddenly turned down Fear Street. "Let's go home just for a second," he said. "Maybe Farraday left a message on the answering machine or something."

"Sure. Good idea," I agreed.

"Oh, no. Cara, look—"

I followed Mark's eyes. The gray van was parked a block from our house.

"It's back," Mark said, speeding past it. I couldn't see if Murdoch was inside it or not.

We pulled up the drive. "That's strange," I said. "Some of the upstairs lights are on. I didn't turn those on."

"Neither did I," Mark said warily. "Let's see what's going on. Maybe it's Roger."

We crept in through the back door. I closed it quietly behind us. Then we walked to the front steps. "Hey, Roger? You home?" I called.

We climbed the stairs. The lights up to the attic had been turned on. "Hey, Roger! You up there?"

Silence.

"Did he turn on all the lights and then leave?" Mark asked.

"He's never done that before," I said. "Let's go upstairs and check out his room."

I led the way. The stairs groaned and squeaked loudly beneath us. "Roger? Roger?"

The light was on in his room. The door was half-open. It was about twenty degrees warmer up here. I pushed the door open wider and walked in. Since I was the first one in the room, I was the first one to see Roger.

I wanted to scream, but no sound came out of my mouth.

I thought I was going to faint. Everything went white for a second or two. Then the colors returned.

And there was Roger sitting at his desk, slumped forward, his head facedown, his arms hanging at his sides, hands down on the floor. An arrow was stuck in his back just below his neck. His shirt was soaked with dark red blood.

I took a step to the side so that Mark could get into the small room. My sneakers squished on the carpet. I looked down to see why. Roger's blood had soaked the rug. I was standing in it.

"Oh, no! I don't believe it!" Mark cried. He put an arm around my shoulder, more to hold himself up than to comfort me. My legs were trembling. My heart was pounding like crazy.

There were arrows scattered across the blood-soaked rug.

"He—he's dead," Mark cried. "But why?"

Suddenly, the door to the room swung in, bumping Mark and me hard. Farraday stepped in front of us. He had been hiding behind the door the whole time.

"Oh!" I cried out.

Farraday was holding Mark's bow. He blocked the doorway and glared at Mark accusingly. "This your weapon, son?" he growled. "Why'd you kill him?"

chapter

21

I stared at Cara and my mind just went blank. At first I thought maybe Farraday was kidding.

But when he didn't take his eyes off my face, just stared at me, holding up my bow like that, I realized he was serious. He was accusing me of killing Roger!

"Now, wait a minute—" I started. My knees felt weak. The tiny room was tilting, first one way then the other. I looked down. My sneakers were soaked with Roger's blood.

Farraday put a hand on my shoulder. "Don't say anything, son. First I have to read you your rights."

I saw his lips moving, but I couldn't hear a word he said. I guess I was in some kind of shock.

"Mark didn't kill Roger!" Cara's angry voice burst into my thoughts. "That's crazy!"

"She's right!" I cried, finally finding my voice. "I didn't kill him. No way! Why would I kill him?"

Farraday kept his hand on my shoulder. He tossed down the bow. "Easy now. Take it easy," he said softly. He started to guide me out of the room. "Let's all just stay calm. A murder has been committed here." He stared at Cara as if trying to read some answers in her eyes. "A murder has been committed with Mark's weapon, and—"

"It's not a weapon!" I cried. I didn't recognize my own voice. It sounded so frightened, so strained.

"Let's go downstairs. We'll sit down and discuss this calmly," Farraday said. He kept his hand on my shoulder as if guiding me, and followed us down the stairs.

I can't describe what I was thinking as I entered the living room. My thoughts were just a wild jumble. Nothing made any sense. Was Roger really dead? Was he killed by my bow and arrow? Who would have done it? Were they trying to make it look as if I did it?

Cara and I were about to sit down on the couch when we saw the living-room door swing open. Murdoch burst in, a pistol in his hand.

He stared in surprise at Farraday. "Who the hell are you?" he cried. "Everybody against the wall! Move!" He was waving his pistol.

"That's him!" Cara screamed. "That's the one who was meeting with Roger!"

Farraday drew a pistol and fired three shots. All three of them hit Murdoch in the chest. His eyes rolled up, he uttered a voiceless cry, and his knees buckled. He fell face forward onto the hallway tiles.

"Oh no, oh no, oh no!" Cara covered her face with her hands.

Farraday moved forward quickly and put a comforting arm around her shoulder. "It's okay now," he said softly. "It's okay now."

I was feeling pretty weird. The floor seemed to tilt and roll. Two dead men. Two. Right in our house. Two people killed. The blood . . . so much blood . . .

Before I realized it, Farraday had an arm around me, too. He was leading Cara and me back to the living-room couch. "It's okay now," he kept repeating softly.

Cara and I sat on opposite ends of the couch. Cara still covered her face. I looked up at Farraday. The room was still tilting crazily. I kept hearing the gunshots again and again, kept seeing Murdoch let out that silent cry and tumble down to the floor.

"You two sit still and get yourselves together," Farraday said softly. He scratched the side of his face, then replaced the pistol in his holster.

He walked back over to Murdoch, rolled him over onto his back, squatted down low beside the body, and stared into his face. "So you saw this guy with Roger?" he asked.

"Yes," Cara said, looking down at the floor. "I saw them together."

"Now maybe we can start to piece this all together and find out what they did to your parents," Farraday said. He groaned loudly as he climbed to his feet.

He picked up the phone on the desk. "I'm just going to call for backups," he said. "My guys'll be here before you know it. They'll clean everything up. Don't move. Just take deep breaths and try to get calm. I didn't figure you for a killer, son."

He walked over to the phone on the desk and dialed the police station. "Yeah, Schmidt. It's me. I'm on

Fear Street. Right. Burroughs. Need some help here. I've got two down. Too late for the ambulance. Yeah. Yeah. Bring 'em. And tell 'em to step on it, okay? Right.''

He replaced the receiver and walked back over to us. He looked eight feet tall standing right above us. Cara was sitting with her hands tightly knotted in her lap. I was just trying to keep the room steady.

"You kids have been through a bad time," Farraday said, looking down at us. "But the worst is over. I think we're going to get to the bottom of things now. How are you feeling?"

"Pretty bad," Cara said. "I've never seen anyone . . . dead before."

I got up unsteadily, holding on to the side of the couch.

"Where are you going, Mark?" Farraday asked, helping me up.

"Just into the kitchen. My mouth is so dry. I just want to get a drink of water."

"Yeah. Bring me one, too," Cara said.

"Okay, go ahead," Farraday said. "But get back here. I still have a lot of questions to ask you two."

As I headed to the kitchen, I saw Farraday go over to the front window and look out. "What's keeping my guys?" I heard him ask.

I walked into the kitchen and was crossing to the sink when I noticed something that sent an icy chill down my back. I stopped. I stared at it. I blinked, trying to change it. But it wouldn't change.

My eyes *weren't* playing tricks on me. The wall phone receiver—it was off the hook.

I picked it up and held it to my ear. Silence. I replaced it, then picked it up again.

Silence.

The phone was dead. Still dead.

Farraday had only pretended to call the police station.

chapter

22

So Farraday was a fake, probably not even a policeman at all.

He hadn't called for backups. He had us all alone here now.

He had killed Murdoch right before our eyes. Had he killed Roger, too? Did he plan to do the same to us?

What did he want? Who *was* he?

What was going on?

My head was spinning with all of these questions.

I replaced the receiver and stood there staring at the phone. Dead, dead, dead.

I had to find a way to warn Cara. I had to let her know that Farraday wasn't who he said he was. He was a fake. A very dangerous fake.

"Hey, Mark, where are you?" Farraday called.

I thought of running out the back door, going for help.

But before I could make a move, Farraday appeared in the kitchen. "Did you get your drink?"

"No. I . . . uh . . ."

I poured a glass of water, took a few sips, then carried the rest for Cara. Farraday guided me gently back to the couch.

Cara took the glass gratefully. I stared at her, rolled my eyes toward Farraday. I had to find a way to tell her, had to find a way to make her understand the danger we were in.

"Uh . . . could Cara and I talk together for a moment in the kitchen?" I asked, trying to sound innocent.

Farraday's nostrils flared slightly, as if he were sensing danger. "No, I don't think that will be necessary," he said calmly, smiling at us. He sat down on a low hassock across from us. "We have so much to talk about."

Cara gave me a funny look. I stared back at her. But she didn't understand.

"Let me just ask you both a few questions," Farraday said softly. He gave Cara a reassuring smile. "I'm sure we can prove that Mark had nothing to do with the young man's death upstairs. As soon as we can get some IDs on this man"—he looked back at Murdoch—"and the one upstairs, I think we'll be able to get on the trail of the real killer."

I tried to get Cara's attention, but she was staring at Farraday. "Who are they?" she asked. "Do you think they know where Mom and Dad are?"

Farraday shrugged. "We'll find out."

"What were *you* doing here?" I asked. I wanted to show Cara that I was suspicious of Farraday. I *had* to let her know that he was a phony. But how?

"I came to talk to you two," Farraday said, scratching his cheek. "I saw lights on upstairs. It looked suspicious, so I went up to investigate. I found the young man—Roger—with the arrow in his back. Then I heard voices approaching, so I hid behind the door.''

He seemed so calm, so professional, so nice. I rolled my eyes at Cara. I made a face at her. She didn't see me.

"Now, you've both been through a terrible shock. Do you think you can answer just a few quick questions for me?"

"Yes, I think so," Cara said softly, clasping her hands tightly in her lap.

How could I get her attention? How could I let her know what I'd discovered?

"Where were you two just before you came home?" Farraday asked, looking to the window as if wondering where his men were, the men he had never really called.

"We went to see a man who knew our parents," Cara told him.

"Cara—no!" I shouted. *"Don't tell him anything!"*

Suddenly I realized I had no choice. I had gone too far. I had to take some kind of action. I took a deep breath and lunged at Farraday. I pushed him hard and he fell over backward off the hassock. "Hey!" he cried out angrily.

"Mark! What are you *doing?*" I heard Cara scream.

I leapt on Farraday and reached for his gun, but he twisted out from under me. He shoved me away and jumped to his feet.

The gun was in his hand. "Smooth move, ace," he said, pointing the gun at me. "But not smooth enough. Get back on that couch."

"Mark! What on *earth!*" Cara cried, looking at me as if I were crazy.

All of the friendliness had dropped from Farraday's face. He stared down at us coldly, pointing the gun at us. "So you *do* know things you haven't told me. I think it's time for you to start talking."

Cara's mouth dropped open in shock. "What?"

"I think you heard me," Farraday snapped. "Let's start with the big question. Where are your parents? Tell me now and we will avoid a lot of trouble."

"But we don't know where they are!" Cara screamed. I put a hand on her shoulder to calm her.

"I'm through playing games with you two," Farraday said, and sighed. "Can't you see that I mean business? I've killed two people in your house tonight. Do you really think I wouldn't kill two more?"

"You—you're not a policeman?" Cara stammered.

"Sure I'm a cop," Farraday said bitterly. He stood up. "At least, I *was* a cop. I *was* a cop for sixteen years. But your parents—"

"What about our parents?" I demanded.

"That's my question," he said impatiently. "I've traveled a long way to find your parents. I've waited a long time to pay them a visit." He stood right above us now. "Where are they?"

"We don't know," I said.

"Why did you kill Roger?" Cara demanded.

"He was snooping around too much. I figured I had you fooled, but I wasn't sure about him. So I sneaked in and let him have it." He stared down at Mark. "Nice of you to leave me a weapon right nearby. A weapon that could never be traced to me. He never turned around, never knew what hit him." Farraday shrugged. "No big deal."

He pulled his pistol. "I've fooled around with you two long enough. Who's going to tell me where your parents are?"

"Mark is telling the truth. We don't know," Cara cried.

"I don't believe you. Sorry." Farraday pointed the pistol at Cara's head. "Know something? I'll bet if I shoot one of you, the other one will suddenly remember where your parents are. Shall we try it?"

"No!" Cara screamed.

Farraday moved the gun toward me. "One of you is going to tell me."

"But our parents are missing!" I cried. "We don't know where they are!"

"Which one of you should I shoot?" Farraday asked. "It's too bad, but you're leaving me no choice. I have to shoot one of you."

He moved the pistol back and forth, first pointing it at Cara, then at me.

"I think I'll shoot Mark," he said.

"No!" Cara shouted. "We don't know! Really!"

"Good-bye, Mark." He lowered the pistol toward my head.

I closed my eyes and waited.

One second. Two seconds. Three seconds.

How much would it hurt? Would I really feel it? Would I know when I was hit?

Four seconds. Five seconds. Six seconds.

He didn't shoot. I opened my eyes.

He slowly lowered his pistol.

I felt so dizzy. I was gasping for breath. I looked up, trying to focus.

Farraday was no longer looking at me. He was looking behind me. He looked very unhappy.

"Drop the pistol," a voice called behind us.

I spun around to see who it was.

"Gena!"

Her black hair was all disheveled. There were stains on her blue sweatshirt. Her cheeks were red and puffy, and her eyes looked swollen, as if she'd been crying.

She had an enormous hunting rifle propped against her shoulder. It was aimed at Farraday.

"Who are you? What are you doing here?" Farraday cried, lowering his gun but not dropping it.

Gena ignored him. "Come on, Mark, Cara. We've got to hurry. The meeting is starting. There's no time to waste."

"Meeting?"

"Stay where you are!" Farraday screamed. He started to raise his pistol.

Gena fired the rifle. The blast blew a hole in the wall behind Farraday. He cried out and dropped his gun. He suddenly looked very pale.

"I'll shoot you. I don't care," Gena warned him. The rifle looked as big as she was. She steadied it on her shoulder. "Don't look so shocked," she told me. "My dad took me hunting for the first time when I was four."

"Gena! Where were you?" I asked.

"There's no time to talk," Gena said. She gestured with the rifle. "What are we going to do with him? We've got to hurry!"

"Why don't we lock him in the garage?" Cara

suggested, jumping up. "The garage door has a really good lock on it."

It seemed like a good idea. Gena kept the hunting rifle in Farraday's back as we pushed him outside and then into the garage.

I was surprised to see that it had been snowing. The ground was already covered with white, and it was still coming down, soft, wet flakes.

"You'll regret this," Farraday said. I pulled the door shut and then locked him inside.

"Come on, get your coats! We may already be too late!" Gena cried, lowering the rifle.

A few seconds later, we were hurrying across our backyard, slipping over the powdery snow. "We'll head through the woods," Gena said. She started running, ignoring the slipperiness of the ground.

Cara and I had to run to catch up. "Where've you been? What happened?" I asked.

"At my cousin's," she replied, her breath coming out in small, white puffs of steam. We were in the woods now, and the wind was howling, making the trees bend and crack. "My dad wanted me out of the way. But I hitchhiked back."

"Hitchhiked?" Cara cried.

"I really can't explain. Let's just run. I hope . . . I hope we can talk later."

"But . . . where are we going? I have to know!"

"It's your parents!" she cried. "We have to get there because . . ." I couldn't hear the rest of it. She had picked up her pace and her words were lost in the wind. I looked back at Cara, who was having trouble keeping up.

The wind was so cold. My face felt raw and frozen

already. I remembered running through these woods last night on my way to Gena's. Was it last night? I flashed back on the trap I had fallen in, on the huge dog that attacked me near the clearing, the desperate fight. I remembered the sound of its neck cracking, the confused look it gave me as it slumped silently to the ground.

Now, the soft snow didn't make these woods any less terrifying. I knew there could be more attack dogs here, ready to pounce. And worse evils much worse evils.

What kind of evil were we heading to? What was the meeting Gena was in such a hurry to get to?

I ran until I thought my lungs would burst. Then we walked quickly, pushing the low tree limbs and tall, snow-covered weeds out of our way. "I—I'm too tired," Cara cried. "I don't think I—"

"Sshhh," Gena whispered. "We're almost there."

Up ahead I suddenly saw small yellow lights, moving in and out through the trees. At first I thought they were fireflies, but of course there are no fireflies in winter. "Candles!" I exclaimed out loud.

Again, Gena signaled for quiet. "Don't let them hear you," she whispered.

"But where are we?" Cara asked.

I recognized it. We were near the round clearing, the clearing where I had seen all those footprints. And now it was filled with people carrying candles.

"The meeting hasn't started yet. We're in time," Gena whispered.

"What meeting?" I insisted. Again she ignored me.

"Follow me. My house is just beyond those trees. I know where my dad keeps some robes."

Robes?

Candles and robes?

"Whoa," I said, and held her back by the arm. "I'm not going another step until you tell me what's going on."

She put her hand over mine. Despite the cold, her hand was burning hot. "Mark, please . . . Don't you want to get your parents back?"

chapter

23

I could feel the danger like shock waves in the air. I guess having it so nearby renewed my energy. Running through the woods, so wet, so cold, I told Mark and Gena I didn't think I could make it. I was just too exhausted—and too frightened, I'll admit.

But seeing the dots of yellow light through the trees, then seeing the hooded figures carrying the candles made me forget how awful I felt.

We were careful not to get too close. But I could see them clearly through the trees. They were milling about in the clearing, about two dozen people. They were all wearing dark monk's robes, their faces hidden in the shadows of their hoods. They each carried a long, black candle.

Were my mom and dad there?

Gena motioned for us to stay silent.

We kept low, walking around the circular clearing, following her, our wet sneakers making no sound on the soft, powdery snow. I could hear soft music. It sounded like a flute, maybe a recorder.

"When the music stops, the meeting will begin," Gena whispered.

She led us into a neighbor's backyard. We ducked down low behind a fence and walked quickly past the house to the front yard.

"The robes are down in my basement," Gena whispered, even though no one was near. "We were stupid. We should've brought that man's pistol. We left it in your living room."

Gena led us toward the side of her house. We pressed against the dark side of the house, then slipped into a side door and down to the basement. I could hear voices upstairs, laughter. And I could hear the recorder music, much fainter now, but still playing.

The basement was fully finished. There was a large rec room and several smaller rooms. One of the smaller rooms seemed to be filled to the ceiling with stacks of rifles. Gena led us to a corner closet and pulled us inside before turning on the light. It was empty except for a pile of brown robes against the wall.

Suddenly she grabbed Mark's arm and looked up at him, her face filled with pain, with fear. "I knew my dad was in the Brotherhood," she said. "But I never knew they killed people."

Brotherhood?

Killed people?

"When I found out what the Brotherhood planned to do, Dad made me call you and break up with you," Gena told Mark. "Then he forced me to go to my cousin's, upstate. He didn't want me to interfere. He doesn't believe in killing. But he's too afraid to stop it."

"But I don't understand," I whispered. "What about our parents? Are they—"

"*Shhh.*" We heard footsteps on the basement stairs. "We've got to get out of here." Gena grabbed up three robes from the pile. "Quick. Put this on."

We scrambled into the robes. They were heavier than they looked. They smelled of mothballs and sweat.

"Keep your face hidden under the hood," Gena said, pulling the hood over her head and tightening the belt robe. "Just try to follow what they're doing."

"The rifle—" I said, pointing.

"I—I don't see how I can sneak it out," Gena said. She buried it under the pile of robes. "They'll see it and then it'll all be over. We'll have to think of something else. Come on!"

Now what? I thought. Why are we sneaking into this meeting? What are we going to do?

We walked quickly out of the closet, just as two men stepped down into the basement. I was careful to keep my face away from them as we passed.

"Evening," one of them said pleasantly.

We didn't reply.

We walked quickly across Gena's backyard, and then through the woods to the clearing. The snow had stopped. It was clear and cold. There was no light except for the small dots of candlelight.

I stayed close to Mark. I didn't want to lose sight of him. It would be so easy to get confused since everyone looked alike. Everyone seemed to be milling around, being social. I didn't get close enough to anyone to hear what they were talking about.

I was terribly frightened. My legs didn't want to

cooperate, but I forced myself to keep walking, to keep moving along the edge of the group.

Suddenly Gena thrust a lighted candle in my hand. The candle was narrow and black. I tried to hold it steady, but my hand was trembling. I hoped no one would notice.

Suddenly, the music stopped. I still couldn't see where it was coming from.

The hooded figures became silent. They began walking into the woods. The Fear Street woods.

How long had these Brotherhood meetings taken place in these woods? How many stories of terror had been created by these Brotherhood members? What did they plan to do tonight?

I tried to force myself to stop asking all these questions, but it was impossible.

The wind blew my hood back. I quickly reached up and pulled it down over my forehead.

"Line up," Gena whispered.

I grabbed Mark's hand. It was ice-cold. I didn't want to get separated. The hooded figures seemed to be forming two lines as they moved toward the edge of the clearing. When everyone was in line, they stopped moving. Now everyone turned in and began to form a circle.

The candles bobbed and flickered. Now they formed a perfect circle of light.

Two hooded figures stepped into the center of the circle. They were holding their candles up close to their faces, and I gasped as I realized they were wearing masks.

White monkey masks—grinning white monkey masks.

They looked just like the tiny white monkey head that Mark and I had found in Mom and Dad's bed.

A third figure, his face hidden in the darkness of his hood, stepped forward.

All was silent. The wind had stopped. No one murmured or said a word.

The man stepped up to the two masked figures. He placed a hand on each mask. And then with one sudden movement, ripped off the white monkey masks.

In the flickering candlelight, I recognized my mom and dad at once.

I looked at Mark. He saw them, too. And I knew that he realized at the same time I did that Mom and Dad must be the leaders of the Brotherhood!

chapter
24

*I*t had to be a dream, just a bad dream. The snow. The dark woods. The people in their brown robes and hoods. The black candles. The circle of tiny lights. And then my mom and dad in the middle of the circle, wearing white monkey masks.

I looked at Cara. Her face had no expression on it at all. It was too much to register. It was too impossible, too weird, too unreal.

Is this why Mom and Dad had abandoned us? To come to the woods and lead this weird cult?

When they said they had club meetings on Thursday nights, were they actually out here in their robes and masks doing—doing what?

What did they do? Were they *witches,* or something?

I thought of all the moving we'd done; a new place, a new house every year or so. My parents must have been moving to start new cult chapters. They weren't computer installers. That was just a cover-up for their real jobs—cult leaders!

I thought I was going to be sick. Our lives had all been a lie. Our parents had lied to us about everything. And then they had left us without a word, abandoned us for the Brotherhood!

I looked back at Cara. She was staring straight ahead; so much fear in her eyes, so much horror.

What was going to happen to us? Why had Gena brought us here?

What were we supposed to *do?*

Suddenly the circle of hooded figures moved in closer. So Gena, Cara, and I moved closer, too.

I realized there was a large, flat tree stump near the center of the circle. The hooded figure who had ripped the masks off my parents led them to the tree stump.

A gust of cold wind came up and blew his hood off. I saw his short, dark hair and heavy, black glasses. I recognized him immediately. It was Mr. Marcus, the big cheese at Cranford.

So this is why he lied to us, I thought. Mom and Dad probably *told* him to lie to us, to tell us they weren't there. Mom and Dad didn't want to see us anymore. They were too busy leading these robed weirdos!

"Now we are ready!" Marcus shouted, not bothering to pull his hood back on. "We of the White Monkey are ready to take back the America that is ours! For too long we have stood by while others determined our nation's fate. No longer! No longer! Soon we shall rise up . . . and take back *by force* what is ours!"

He kept his arms raised high as he talked. "The government of this nation has given in to criminals, but we are going to change that! Our revenge will be swift and our justice will reign. No criminal will be safe once our army has proven its capabilities. We will take back our community—and our nation from the criminal element—by force!''

The robed figures, except for my parents, cheered behind their hoods.

"No to the courts! No to the weak-kneed police! *Yes* to the Brotherhood!" Marcus screamed, and another cheer echoed through the woods.

As the cheer died down, Marcus lowered his arms and looked down at my parents. "And they who have betrayed us shall be the first to feel the vengeance!" he shouted.

Betrayed us? What did he mean?

He raised his hands again. Now I saw a long-bladed knife in his hand.

"The Brotherhood of the White Monkey is always merciless to traitors!" Marcus shouted. The crowd cheered.

"The vengeance is always swift!" Marcus shouted, and everyone cheered again.

The wind came up and almost blew back my hood. I grabbed it and held it with both hands. I hoped no one had seen my face.

When I looked back to the center of the circle, a hooded man stepped forward and forced my dad down onto his knees. He was pushing his head down onto the flat tree stump.

"We've got to do something—now," Gena whispered to me.

Marcus raised his knife above my dad's head. "The sacrifice will be done!" he shouted. "This is the way *our* army will administer justice!"

Ohh! I uttered a silent gasp. My head throbbed. I felt a shock of fear run down my spine.

Why had it taken me so long to realize—my parents weren't the leaders of the Brotherhood. My parents were about to be *murdered* by them! And they couldn't run or fight—because the hooded man had a gun on them.

Marcus pressed his knee down onto my dad's back. He raised his knife above his head again. "Will you confess that you are a traitor to the White Monkey?" he bellowed.

"Confess!" someone in the crowd shouted.

The wind swirled. Again, I grabbed my hood. Cara squeezed my hand. "Mark," she whispered, "what are we going to do?"

"He will not confess!" Marcus cried. "The vengeance will be ours!"

He lowered the knife over my dad's head.

"No! NO! Don't kill him!" my mom screamed. She grabbed Marcus and tried to pull back the hand with the knife.

He pushed my mom away and the hooded man grabbed her from behind. Then Marcus turned back to my dad, whose head was still down against the tree stump.

"The vengeance will not be slowed!" he cried.

I knew I had to act now if I was ever going to do anything. But what could I do without a weapon of any kind? If I tried to run up and leap on Marcus, I'd only be stopped by someone in the cult, or I'd be shot.

"Mark . . ." Cara said. Her eyes were brimming with tears.

She brushed against me, and I felt something in my jeans pocket. Quickly I reached under the robe, and I pulled it out of my pocket.

It was the little white monkey head, hard and cold. The little white monkey head I had picked up off the floor in Gena's room.

I didn't think. I didn't aim. I just heaved it at Marcus, as hard as I could.

I wanted to hit him right between the eyes. If I stunned him, it might give my parents a chance to get away.

He turned in my direction just as I heaved the tiny white monkey head. His hood was back on his shoulders. His face was revealed, vulnerable.

Perfect, I thought. Perfect.

The white monkey head sailed through the darkness.

It sailed right over his shoulder.

I missed.

I missed by several inches.

"Who threw that?" Marcus bellowed.

He was staring right at me.

chapter
25

I saw Mark throw something. And then I saw Mr. Marcus spin around and come toward Mark.

I guessed that Mark had missed. I couldn't really see in the darkness.

"Who threw that?" Marcus shouted.

He took two or three steps toward Mark.

Mark started to back up.

This was all the distraction my parents needed.

Suddenly my mom pulled away from the hooded man, knocking his gun to the ground. My dad leapt up and shoved Marcus hard from behind.

Marcus cried out in surprise as he fell facedown in the snow and the knife bounced out of his hand.

All of the rest of the hooded cult members seemed totally confused and surprised. Some started to run away. But most of them just froze there in the circle.

My dad dived for the gun and came up with it quickly. He kicked the knife out of Marcus's hand as my mother scrambled to his side.

Dad pressed the gun against Marcus's neck. "Don't anybody move, or I'll blow his head off!" he screamed. "You're all under arrest. FBI!"

Ignoring Dad's threat, the hooded Brotherhood members began to scatter, fleeing into the woods.

Mark and I threw back our hoods and went running up to our parents. Mom saw us first. "You—you're here!" she cried, and she rushed forward and gathered us both up in a hug. "Oh, I don't believe it! I don't believe it! You're here! You're okay!"

"Get to the house. Call for some assistance. We're a little outnumbered here," Dad shouted, keeping his gun pressed tightly against Marcus's throat.

"Dad, everyone else is getting away," I cried.

"I know who they are. They can't run far," Dad said.

Mom grabbed up the knife, then hurried toward the house.

Dad turned to Mark. "Where'd you ever learn to throw?"

"Sorry," Mark started, then he saw the smile on Dad's face.

"You saved our lives, Mark."

"Actually, Gena did," Mark said. He put his arm around her shoulder.

A big man in a robe walked up slowly, his hands raised above his head in surrender. "I tried to stop them, Greg," he said. It was Dr. Rawlings, Gena's dad. "I did the best I could. But I was afraid—afraid of them, afraid for Gena, afraid for me. At least I persuaded them not to go after your kids."

"I'll remember that," Dad told him, his hard expression not changing. "But now I'm afraid I have to put you under arrest. How'd you ever get involved in the Brotherhood in the first place, Rawlings?"

Gena's dad uttered a weary sigh. "I believed in what Marcus and the others were saying—at first. I believed that we had to do something about crime, that we had to make this country safe again. But I didn't know they were going to stockpile weapons, to take the law into their own hands . . . to kill people. I wanted to get out, Greg. But I was scared, scared they'd come after *me*."

Marcus scowled and spit into the snow. "You're a coward, Rawlings. You'll die for your cowardice. The vengeance of the White Monkey will be swift," he muttered, and looked away.

Dad ignored him and turned to Gena. "I think I owe you an apology, for trying to keep you and Mark apart," he said. He shoved Marcus toward the house. "Come on. Move. I want to get out of this robe. I never did like going outside in a bathrobe."

We started walking toward the house. "I'm so sorry. I'll bet you two have been worried sick," Dad said.

"That's a bit of an understatement," I told him. I could hear police sirens in the distance. Mom must have made her call.

"Where's Roger?" Dad asked. "Isn't he here, too?"

"Uh . . . Roger is dead," I said.

Dad stopped walking. His eyes narrowed. He shook his head. "No. Oh, no. Roger was one of our best agents. After the Brotherhood found out your mom and I were agents, I was worried they'd come after Roger—and you."

"A man named Murdoch was killed, too," I told him.

Another look of shock and sadness crossed Dad's face. "Murdoch was our field director here. The Brotherhood killed him, too?"

"Not the Brotherhood," I said. "A man named Farraday."

"Who? Farraday?" Dad's face filled with shock and disbelief. He stared past me, thinking hard. "Farraday? He's here? He's out of prison? What's he doing here?"

"Who is he, Dad?" I asked.

"He was a cop, Mark. A bent cop. Your mother and I were responsible for his getting sent up on racketeering charges. He killed Roger and Murdoch?"

"We thought he was a real cop," Cara said. "He had a police radio and everything."

"Anyone can buy a radio that gets the police band," Dad explained.

"Farraday was looking for you," I said. "We locked him in the garage."

Tears formed in the corners of Dad's eyes, the first tears I had ever seen him shed. "I'm so sorry," he said. "I never meant for you two to be involved in any of this."

"It's over now," I said. I hoped against hope that I was right.

We followed Dad to the Rawlingses' house, feeling very relieved but still terribly confused.

chapter

26

"We were in a terrible fix," Mom said to Cara and me. "We didn't want to lie to you, but we didn't want you involved. We just thought you'd worry about us all the time if you knew we were FBI agents."

We were home, all four of us together. The police had come to collect Farraday and remove poor Roger's body. And so it was just us four. We were so happy. Dad made hot chocolate and we sat around the kitchen table and talked.

"So you never were computer experts?" Cara asked. She looked very confused.

"Yes, sure we are. We know a lot about computers," Dad said. "But we know a lot more about subversive groups."

Mom sighed. "It isn't pleasant work. I guess you saw that tonight."

"And that's why we move so much?" I asked.

Mom nodded. "We tried to give you normal childhoods, as normal as possible. That's why we didn't tell you the truth."

"Up till now, we've been lucky," Dad said.

"We're still lucky," Mom interrupted. "Lucky to be alive."

"But this was the first time our cover was blown," Dad said, twirling the cup around between his hands. "These White Monkey followers really were going to kill us."

"But why, Dad?" I asked. "Why did all these people do what Marcus told them to?"

"He was a forceful, charismatic leader," Dad said. "And he told them what they wanted to hear. He made them believe that he could lead them to a better way of life."

"Where were you all this time?" I asked.

"Marcus kept us prisoner in the basement at Cranford for three days," Mom said. "He had to wait till the meeting night to execute us."

"Did you really work at Cranford?" I asked.

"Yes, we did," Mom said. "That's how we infiltrated the Brotherhood. Marcus and his crew planned a complete takeover of Cranford. That would have given them access to a lot of top-secret government weapons."

"I think they really would've used those weapons," Dad said, shaking his head. "If they'd gotten half a chance."

"But it was the Burroughs family to the rescue!" Mom cried, and we all cheered.

"Mark, I hope you understand why we tried to warn you about Gena," Dad explained, putting his hand on my arm. "There we were, trying to get enough evidence to arrest the Brotherhood members, and we knew that her dad was one of them. I tried to warn you away, but of course I couldn't tell you the reason.''

''I guess Gena surprised everyone,'' I said. I wondered what she was doing now.

''She's a very brave girl,'' Dad said.

''And what about Roger? He wasn't really our cousin? He was working for you?'' Cara asked.

''Yes. He was one of our agents.''

''He acted so weird after you disappeared,'' Cara said. ''We didn't know what to think.''

''He must have been frantically trying to find us,'' Dad said. ''He and Murdoch. They were probably searching everywhere.'' He looked at Mom, who looked away sadly.

We drank our hot chocolate. There wasn't much else to say. All of the questions had been answered. Well, almost all.

''What happens next?'' I asked.

''We move on to the next case,'' Mom said. ''Only this time it will be different. Our cover has been blown with our own family.''

By Saturday, Mom and Dad were already packing cartons, preparing for our next move. The doorbell rang just after breakfast. It was Gena. Behind her, I saw a taxi in the drive.

''Hi. Come in,'' I said.

''I can't. I'm on my way to the airport.''

''Where are you going?''

''Detroit. My mother is there. I'm going to live with her . . . while my dad . . . you know.''

I took her hand. ''Are you okay?''

''Yeah. I guess. It's going to take a long time for

everything that happened to sink in. And I—I'm going to miss you.''

"I'm—I mean we're leaving, too, I don't know where," I said, "but I'll write to you."

"Good. I'll write, too." The taxi driver blew his horn. He was anxious to leave. Gena reached up on tiptoes and kissed me. Her face was cold, but her mouth was warm. It was a long, wonderful kiss. I knew I'd never forget it.

Then she slipped a small package into my hand, turned, and ran to the taxi without looking back.

I stepped out onto the front porch and watched her leave. She waved, and then the taxi was gone.

I looked at the package. It was a little box, the kind jewelry comes in. I pulled it open. Inside was a little white monkey head with rhinestone eyes.

Why on earth did she give me this? I thought.

I pulled it out of the box. Something was stuck inside the grinning mouth. It took me a while to get it out. It was a narrow strip of paper. I unrolled the strip of paper. Gena had written her Detroit address and a message on it: Can you keep a secret? I love you. Gena.

I rolled up the slip of paper and stuffed it back into the monkey's mouth. I held the white monkey in my hand. For the first time, it didn't feel cold. It felt very warm. I tossed it up into the air, caught it, and stuffed it into my jeans pocket.

I wouldn't need it to remember Gena and my stay on Fear Street, but I planned on keeping it a long time anyway.

About the Author

R. L. STINE is the author of more than 70 books of humor, adventure and mystery for young readers. In recent years, he has been concentrating on scary thrillers, such as this one.

For ten years, he was editor of *Bananas,* a national humor magazine for young people. In addition to magazine and book writing, he is currently Head Writer of the children's TV show, "Eureeka's Castle."

He lives in New York City with his wife Jane and son Matthew.